Frankenstein Meets The Hunchback of Notre-Dame

also by Frank J. Morlock

Lord Ruthven the Vampire
(*John William Polidori &*
adapted from Charles Nodier and Eugène Scribe)

The Return of Lord Ruthven
(*adapted from Alexandre Dumas*)

Arsène Lupin vs. Sherlock Holmes: The Stage Play
(*adapted from Victor Darlay & Henry de Gorsse*)

Frankenstein Meets The Hunchback of Notre-Dame

by

Charles Nodier,
Antoine Nicolas Béraud
& Jean Toussaint Merle

and

Victor Hugo,
Paul Foucher & Paul Meurice

adapted in English

by

Frank J. Morlock

A Black Coat Press Book

Acknowledgements: We are indebted to Jackie Stanton for typing the plays and David McDonnell for proofreading the typescript.

To Dan, Donna and Judy Woloshen for many years of friendship.

Frankenstein created by Mary Shelley.
The Hunchback of Notre-Dame created by Victor Hugo.

Visit our website at www.blackcoatpress.com

ISBN 1-932983-38-4. First Printing. June 2005. Published by Black Coat Press, an imprint of Hollywood Comics.com, LLC, P.O. Box 17270, Encino, CA 91416.

Table of Contents

The Monster and the Magician, or Frankenstein Revisited

A Fantastic Melodrama in Three Acts
by

Charles Nodier, Antoine Nicolas Béraud & Jean Toussaint Merle

inspired by the novel of
Mary Shelley

translated and adapted by
Frank J. Morlock

Introduction

On that fabled stormy night of 1816 at the Villa Diodati near Lake Geneva, Switzerland, George Gordon, Lord Byron and John William Polidori created the handsome vampire Lord Ruthven,[1] and Mary Shelley created the dread Frankenstein and his immortal Monster.

After Shelley's novel was published in 1818, it was quickly dramatized in England in 1823 by Richard Brinsley Peake. The French play entitled *Le Monstre et le Magicien* (*The Monster and the Magician, or Frankenstein Revisited*), translated here, however, did not appear until 1826. It was credited, in various combinations, to the trio of Charles Nodier, Antoine Nicolas Béraud and Jean Toussaint Merle.

Charles Nodier and Antoine Nicolas Béraud:

Charles Nodier (1780-1844) was born in Besançon in Eastern France, also Victor Hugo's birthplace. He witnessed first hand the bloody events of the French Revolution as a teenager in Strasbourg in 1794, where his father had sent him to learn Greek from Euloge Schneider, the leading Jacobin of that town, a man noted for both his cruelty and his corruption. When Alexandre Dumas wrote *Les Blancs et les Bleus* (*The Whites and the Blues*, 1867), he drew from Nodier's personal expe-

---

[1] See *Lord Ruthven the Vampire*, 1-932983-10-4 and *The Return of Lord Ruthven*, 1-932983-11-2, both published by Black Coat Press, 2004.

rience of that ghastly period of French history known as the Terror.

Nodier became an opponent of Napoleon and fell foul of the authorities for having written a skit on the Emperor, but after his fall, Nodier emerged as an early Romantic writer. He began his career by penning popular Gothic novels such as *Les Proscrits* (*The Proscribed*, 1802) and *Le Peintre de Salzbourg* (*The Painter of Salzburg*, 1803). In 1820, he wrote the play *Lord Ruthven le Vampire* based on the Polidori story.[2] In 1821, he wrote the classic *Smarra ou les Démons de la Nuit* (*Smarra, or The Demons of the Night*), a collection of terrifying dream-based tales.

In 1824, Nodier became Head Librarian of the Arsenal Library in Paris, where, with his daughter as hostess, he held very influential dinners for the young Romantics: Victor Hugo, Alexandre Dumas, George Sand, Alfred de Musset, Alfred de Vigny, etc.

Antoine Nicolas Béraud was one of Nodier's protégés and an occasional collaborator. *The Monster and the Magician* was, in fact, first credited to Jean Toussaint Merle (see below) and "Antony," a pseudonym commonly used by Nodier and Béraud to sign their collaborations.

Nodier is also reputed to have been the head of the Priory of Sion from about 1800 until his death, when Victor Hugo allegedly became the head of this shadowy organization.

At the present time, Nodier's work is enjoying a revival in France, although mostly confined to his tales of supernatural events. Whether he was actually involved in the Priory of Sion is open to question, but it is interesting

---

[2] Included in *Lord Ruthven the Vampire*, q.v.

to note that he wrote a history of secret organizations in the French Army.

Jean Toussaint Merle:

Jean Toussaint Merle (1785-1852) was born in Montpellier. After a tour in Napoleon's army in Spain, he arrived in Paris in 1808 and delivered himself to literature. He worked for a large number of famous newspapers such as *Le Mercure de France* and *La Gazette de France*. As a critic, he was witty and moderate and did not make many enemies.

In 1822, Merle became director of the Theater of the Porte Saint-Martin. During this period, he made several trips to England to study the traditions and resources of the English Theater. He was the first to invite a troupe of British players to France. There is little doubt that he co-wrote, or more likely, rewrote and possibly commissioned Nodier and Béraud's *The Monster and the Magician,* in which the renowned English mime Thomas Potter Cooke was invited to play the role of the Monster.

Merle routinely claimed part of the writing credit for his productions, presumably for alterations made in the course of his work as producer and director. Given that the plays he staged tended to be taken from pre-existing novels, he probably regarded the whole adaptation process as serial improvisation.

Dumas, in his autobiography, wrote that he went to the Théâtre de la Porte Saint-Martin on his first night in Paris to see Nodier's *Lord Ruthven le Vampire* and found himself sitting next to an irascible old man who kept making rude comments about the play. That man turned out to be Nodier himself, presumably disapproving of Merle's amendments to his version of the script.

Dumas, of course, later got to do his own version of the same play.[3]

In the end, Merle did not have the administrative talent to run a theater and, in 1826, he resigned and resumed his career as a writer. He married the actress Marie Dorval, who had starred in *The Monster and the Magician*. He was supposedly of a likable indolence, which was the main trait of his character. He wrote several historical works about French military operations in Africa and about 120 plays, mostly rewrites and/or collaborations with others.

The Monster and the Magician:

The Monster and the Magician was first performed on June 10, 1826, at the Théâtre de la Porte Saint-Martin in Paris and ran for 96 performances. It featured music by M. Alexandre, a ballet by M. Coraly and sets by Mrrs. Lefebvre & Tomkins. The Monster was played by British actor Thomas Potter Cooke and Cecilia by Marie Dorval, the then-perfect incarnation of the passionate and deeply tragic Romantic heroine.

Nodier had already dramatized Polidori's Lord Ruthven in 1821 before turning his hand to Shelley's Frankenstein. Yet, he appears much less at ease in this work than he was with the Byronesque vampire. Strangely, Thomas Potter Cooke who played Ruthven on the London stage, played the part of the Monster in Nodier's version.

The play itself seems rather tame by modern standards, or even when compared with Nodier's own vampire play. But it must be recognized as an innovation

[3] *The Return of Lord Ruthven*, q.v.

when it occurred. The Monster has no name and the period and place of the action has been transferred from the Swiss Alps of the 1770s to Venice in the 16th century. The creator is no longer Victor Frankenstein, a scientist, but Zametti, a celebrated alchemist. So it is magic, proto-science, not modern science, that creates the Monster with no name. Also, in *The Monster and the Magician*, unlike in Shelley's original work, the Creature never speaks.

Thomas Potter Cooke and Marie Dorval

Curiously, both of these changes anticipate the appearance of Dr. Pretorius in the 1935 *The Bride of Frankenstein* and the widely popular Boris Karloff interpretation. One wonders whether these changes were made to avoid charges of plagiarism, or to better fit the tastes and preconceptions of the French public? Was alchemy intrinsically more believable than electricity when it came to creating life? Where the English audience was embracing the future and the wonders it promised, while the French felt more comfortable with the well-worn traditions of the past? And the pantomime Monster may well have been tailored by Merle to entice and better fit Cooke's mime talent. However, one also notes that Nodier later wrote a short work intended simply for pantomime alone.

Frankenstein in France:

Although the French have had lots of "sacred monsters" in their past, and there are plenty of French-language works dealing with vampires, werewolves and other monsters, the character of Frankenstein does not seems to have received more than a flickering attention.

Compared to the abundant use and reuse of Mary Shelley's immortal creature in the English and American media, the French adaptations or spin-offs of *Frankenstein* are relatively few.

The most notable is a series of six novels penned by renowned film writer Jean-Claude Carrière under the nom-de-plume of "Benoît Becker" and published by Fleuve Noir in their "Angoisse" horror imprint in 1957 and 1958. These six pastiches continue the adventures of Mary Shelley's Monster after the end of her novel. They are: *La Tour de Frankenstein* (*The Tower of Frankenstein*), *Le Pas de Frankenstein* (*The Step of Frankenstein*), *La Nuit de Frankenstein* (*The Night of Frankenstein*), *Le Sceau de Frankenstein* (*The Seal of Frankenstein*), *Frankenstein Rôde* (*Frankenstein Prowls*) and *La Cave de Frankenstein* (*The Cellar of Frankenstein*).[4]

---

[4] More details about these six novels, and their 1972 comic-book adaptations, can be found in Jean-Marc & Randy Lof-

Carrière's approach to the character was startingly different from both the Universal and Hammer versions. In his novels, he christened the Monster "Gouroull" and followed his footsteps, as he made his way back from the Arctic to Scotland, and then to Germany and Switzerland, from the late 1800s to the 1920s. Unlike its predecessors, Carrière's Monster was a ruthless, demoniacal thing, the very incarnation of evil. His yellow, unblinking eyes hid a cunning, inhuman intelligence. The Monster barely spoke, but used his razor-sharp teeth to slit his victims' throats.

Carrière emphasized the physical inhumanity of the creature: the Monster did not breathe, its skin was white as chalk but strangely impervious to flames, its strength and speed were prodigious, what ran in its veins was not blood but ichor, and it had no normal heartbeat; even its thought process was shown to be alien.

As far as film and television are concerned, other than a few comical shorter features, such as the classic 1952 *Torticola contre Frankensberg*, a surreal parody of Gothic horror films, there are really only two major French adaptations of Mary Shelley's classic, neither of which is very convincing.

A 1974 *Frankenstein* made-for-television feature, directed by Bob Thénault and written by François Chevallier, cast Gérard Berner as the hapless Victor Frankenstein and Gérard Boucaron as the Monster, now christened Frobelius. In it, after having been expelled from the university and repudiated by his family, Victor conducts his experiments on Frobelius, a retarded man.

---

ficier's *Shadowmen 2: Heroes and Villains from French Comics*, ISBN 0-9740711-8-8 (Black Coat Press, 2004).

After the latter dies in a mountain accident, Victor brings him back to life.

Worse was *Frankenstein '90*, an 1984 feature film comedy by otherwise serious director Alain Jessua, co-written with Paul Gégauff, which cast the noted French comedian Jean Rochefort as Victor Frankenstein and French pop singer Eddy Mitchell as his Creature. Here, Shelley's myth is the pretextv for a lame romantic comedy in which the Creature falls in love with his creator's fiancée and vice-versa.

If popular psychology is correct, Frankenstein evokes a fear of rationality and science running amok. To judge by its enduring popularity, that terror still troubles the Anglo-Saxon psyche to this day. Perhaps the French are just less inclined towards fear of science and rationality than the English? Why that would be the case is not clear, since the English blame excessive rationalism for the Terror under the French Revolution, not to mention Marxism and Stalinism. For reasons best known to themselves, the French have not been very moved by such arguments, which may account for the relative short popularity of *Frankenstein* in France.

Characters

The Monster
Zametti, a celebrated Venetian alchemist
Olben, a blind old man, father of Janskin and Cecilia
Janskin, the leader of a band of Gypsies
Cecilia, Olben's daughter and Zametti's fiancée
Pietro, Zametti's servant
Antonio, Zametti's son, age eight
Petrusco, a Gypsy
The Genie of the Black Rock
Gypsies, Villagers, Zametti's servants, etc.

The action takes place in the 16th century on the shores of the Adriatic, near Venice.

Act I

Scene I

The stage represents a somber forest. To the right, midway back in the midst of a thicket of trees, near a cavern, is an ancient, half-destroyed sarcophagus made of jet-black stone, surrounded by thick bushes. To the left, close to the audience, is an oddly-shaped piece of stone upon which one can sit.

The end of the Overture has depicted a storm. AT RISE, thunder grumbles and one sees light flashing, shining through the thick foliage of the dark forest. The stage is in the deepest obscurity. Janskin advances slowly, furtively, at the head of his band of Gypsies, Petrusco right behind him. He seems to be seeking his way.

PETRUSCO: What a frightful storm!
JANSKIN: Yes, it caught us quite unprepared. But should poor devils of Gypsies such as we complain of the weather? We're used to such rain and storm.

(*The Gypsies stop for a moment; some of them go and sit on the sarcophagus at the right.*)

PETRUSCO: Where are we?
JANSKIN (*looking around*): I'm not sure yet...

(*A lightning bolt shines. In its light, Janskin notices the ancient sarcophagus; he rushes towards those who are seated on it.*)

JANSKIN: Get away from there, you fools!
PETRUSCO: Why?
JANSKIN: Why? Why? Because this place is cursed!

(*All the Gypsies react with terror. Those surrounding the sarcophagus quickly distance themselves from it.*)

PETRUSCO (*emotionally*): Tell us, Janskin... Are we going to stop here?
JANSKIN: No. I'm the only one who'll be staying. You all–leave! You'll wait for me by the big rock near Olben's thatched cottage.
PETRUSCO: Ah! The old blind man–Understood–but what about you? Why aren't you coming with us?
JANSKIN: Questions again! (*abruptly*) I'm waiting for someone here. (*to the Gypsies*) Get going and be careful not to be caught by the Police–you know they're not our friends. Go!

(*On Janskin's order, the Gypsies make off and disappear.*)

JANSKIN: How strange fate is! I was once the son of wealthy Tyrolians, yet now I'm only the leader of a miserable band of Gypsies. That's the result of my many sins. After having reduced my father to misery, I ran wildly through the world–and caroused everywhere, I robbed, I stole and I enjoyed playing with the fate of men. But now I'm weary of this life. I repent it. I want nothing more than to reconcile with my old father. I returned to Tyrol, looking for him, but there, I learned that he had left over a year ago. I sought the help of Zametti, an old friend of my youth. He told me that my father and my sister, Cecilia, had come to live in this county, not far from the shores of the Adriatic. I've seen Zametti again recently. I found out that he secretly loves Cecilia. He wants to marry her. That wedding will serve my cause. In the midst of all the rejoicing, I will show myself to my father. He won't be able to refuse to forgive me. Then, I can say goodbye forever to the Gypsies whom I command. I want to end my life as an honest man. Still, I'm uneasy... Zametti has now dedicated himself to the studies of the works of Paracelsus, Albertus Magnus and Doctor Faustus–cursed works–he has sacrilegious designs. I can say no more. I know he plans to come today to this dark place... I must stop him before he succumbs to Evil. Hark! Someone's coming. Could it be him?

(*Pietro, a box under his arm, enters. He seems seized by some vivid terror.*)

PIETRO: What evil forest! How sinister everything looks. I haven't got one drop of warm blood left in my veins. (*to his master*) Ah, sir, why have we come here?

(*Enter Zametti, somber and preoccupied.*)

ZAMETTI: Shut up!
PIETRO: Some great evil is going to happen to us, I feel it.
ZAMETTI: Quiet, I tell you. (*going to the front of the stone sarcophagus*) Place the box here.
PIETRO (*trembling*): Yes, sir.
JANSKIN (*aside*): It's him!

(*He emerges from the corner where he was hidden.*)

ZAMETTI (*hearing the noise of Janskin's feet*): Some-one's here! (*aloud in a threatening voice*) Who goes there?
JANSKIN (*approaching*): A friend.
ZAMETTI (*upset*): Janskin! What brings you here?
JANSKIN: The desire to see and speak to you.
ZAMETTI: The moment is ill-chosen. Go away!
JANSKIN: No. I choose to stay.
ZAMETTI: What for?
JANSKIN: You'll soon find out. (*gesturing to Pietro to get away*)
PIETRO (*who doesn't understand*): What?
JANSKIN (*aloud*): Leave us!
PIETRO: Where do you want me to go?
JANSKIN: I don't know. Away from us.
PIETRO (*aside*): Hum! This one's got a face well-suited to this God-forsaken place. (*another gesture by Janskin*) I obey, I obey.

(*Pietro goes toward the back; we occasionally lose sight of him.*)

ZAMETTI (*to Janskin*): What do you want with me?
JANSKIN: In the position in which I find myself, I can't see you, except in secret, and for only a moment. Thus, I'm going to hasten to talk plainly. The first time I presented myself before you, I was only able to tell you of my past misfortunes and my hopes for the future. Yet, I was struck by your air of suffering and distress. Since then, I've gathered information. I've followed you and your labors without your suspecting it–and now, I know everything.
ZAMETTI: What do you mean?

JANSKIN: Listen, Zametti. You must realize: the same studies filled our youth. Like you, I was drawn to the Great Work, I sought to discover the Philosopher's Stone, I burned more coal in my furnace than is produced in a year in the Black Forest. I studied it all: chemistry, alchemy, astrology–but after dirtying my hands and tiring my eyes, I became convinced that the best thing was to take men as they are, the weather as it comes, and money for what it's worth. You, on the other hand, are still filled with an ambition that is inflamed further by each new success. You've reached the ends of science. Fatal path! Deplorable talent! That will cause your ruin, and perhaps ours as well.
ZAMETTI: What are you talking about?
JANSKIN: That Hellish sprit that resides here–
ZAMETTI: O Merciful Heaven! You know–
JANSKIN: –Everything! I know that a nefarious Genie dwells in this mysterious and dark forest. Remember: we visited this place in our youth. It is here that you formed your arcane and presumptuous design. Here that you first dared interrogate the Spirits from Beyond. Your plan is already more than half-fulfilled–but trust me, Zametti, stop your mad quest before it is too late.
ZAMETTI: Why do you ask this from me?
JANSKIN: For your own safety, my happiness–that of my sister and my father.
ZAMETTI: I cannot turn away from my path.
JANSKIN: Do you want your ruin and ours?
ZAMETTI: I can't stop–not after so much toilsome labor.
JANSKIN: Content yourself with being the most knowledgeable of men, and don't become the most sinful. My friend, on you depends my fate, that of my father–and of Cecilia!

ZAMETTI: Cecilia!
JANSKIN: You love her and her love is equal to yours. Tomorrow, you will lead her to the altar. Your marriage guarantees the peace of my father's old age and puts an end to my misfortunes. In a few days, we will again be a single family–and our happiness will be your work. I know your soul to be great and generous. Never has any vile calculation directed your thoughts. Friend of all the unfortunate, your fortune is theirs. Everywhere, they bless you, they love you. Your own son, your only son, the first of a first marriage, entrusted to Cecilia's care, repeats your name, the name of his father, with love. But all fear your ambition. Why aren't you content with your fate? Why do you want to penetrate a mystery that Heaven has wisely hidden from the weakness of men?
ZAMETTI: My task must be accomplished. My labors demand an unparalleled result. I won't leave my work unfinished. The Genius of Black Stone will soon grant me a slave submissive to my will. Soon, perhaps, I will insure centuries of glory for myself–and Cecilia.
JANSKIN: My friend, I entreat you, abandon your dire plans. There's still time.
ZAMETTI: Leave me alone!
JANSKIN: At least, before executing them, wait until after you're married to my sister.
ZAMETTI: Why?
JANSKIN (*in an solemn voice*): Her virtues will protect you from the wrath of Heaven.
ZAMETTI: Yes–that could be.
JANSKIN: Swear to me to return to your castle this very night.
ZAMETTI: This very night...
JANSKIN: It must be!
ZAMETTI: I don't know...

JANSKIN: I'm begging you. In the name of our friendship and for the well-being of us all.

(*There is a noise outside. Pietro runs towards it.*)

PIETRO: A man's coming from that direction.
ZAMETTI: Heavens!

(*Petrusco enters, out of breath.*)

PETRUSCO (*to Janskin, in a rapid voice*): The Police are in pursuit of us. Our comrades sent me. You know all the secret paths of this forest. Come, Chief, lead us and guide us out of this accursed place.
JANSKIN: What tragic luck!
PETRUSCO: Hurry! Hurry!
JANSKIN (*to Zametti*): Something dangerous that is my solemn duty has come up. My poor comrades have entrusted me with their safety. I cannot betray their trust. I'm forced to go, Zametti. But, please, swear to me that you will leave this forest instantly.
ZAMETTI (*hesitating*): Well, er–
JANSKIN: I will see you tonight. I hope I have convinced you. Goodbye.

(*Janskin presses Zametti's hand and goes away quickly with Petrusco.*)

PIETRO (*aside, following Janskin with his eyes*): Despite his strange appearance, that man seems to me to have a good heart after all. I wouldn't have been sorry to see him stay. Alas! I'm always afraid when I'm alone with my master... Afraid of seeing some horrible demon suddenly appear.

ZAMETTI (*emerging from his thoughts*): Could Janskin be right? And, indeed, should I fear for Cecilia? Cecilia, adored lover, it's to forever insure your happiness and mine that I wish to possess such a secret. Still, Janskin's fears may have some reality. Let's defer my latest attempt to another day... (*to Pietro*) Let's go, come.
PIETRO (*placing the box back under his arm*): With all my heart.

(*They take a few steps. Suddenly, Zametti stops. He seems undecided for a moment, then returns rapidly.*)

ZAMETTI (*to himself*): No I can't! An imperious desire drags me. Idle terror–so close to the goal to which I aspire–am I perhaps to abandon it forever? No, I shan't! I shan't!
PIETRO (*aside*): Ah! My God, what's the matter with him now?
ZAMETTI (*to himself*): What I plan to do here may cause my ruin. But if I keep it for myself alone–where will be the crime? What have I to worry about? Nothing. Mysterious treasure, I will acquire you and at least my labors will not remain unfulfilled. Yes, it's decided. (*rushing to Pietro and snatching the box from him*) Give this to me, Pietro.
PIETRO (*terrified*): Goodness of Heaven! Sir, what are you doing?
ZAMETTI (*opening the box*): Get out of here!
PIETRO: No, my dear master, no. I can't–I can see that you have some sinister plan. Mercy, let's leave together.
ZAMETTI (*removing several cabalistic instruments from the box*): Go away!

PIETRO: The condition in which I see you now has worried me for days. Your incessant shivering, your gloomy disposition, your pale–
ZAMETTI (*in a terrible voice*): I'm ordering you to leave!
PIETRO: My dear master, in the name of what you hold most dear–
ZAMETTI: So be it then! Stay!

(*He projects his arms towards Pietro and makes a wizardly gesture. Immediately, the servant becomes motionless and dumb, transfixed by the Magician's spell. Zametti then begins his conjurations. Thunder growls, lightning flashes, a subterranean noise is heard. A circle of fire surrounds him.*)

ZAMETTI (*in an imposing voice*): Genie of the Black Stone whom I have subdued by my power, hear my voice and obey! Show yourself!

(*More thunder and lightning. At Zametti's voice, the subterranean uproar increases. The Black Sarcophagus shakes–and in the midst of the flames which surround it, the Genie appears. He holds a jar in his hand.*)

GENIE (*in a gloomy voice, vase in hand*): What do you want from me?
ZAMETTI: That jar that you hold, which contains the reward of my efforts.
GENIE: Fool! Is this what you want?
ZAMETTI: Yes. Give it to me!
GENIE: I know your mad ambition and your insane desires. You have much to fear, wretched human!

ZAMETTI: Don't lecture me. Give me what I want. Now!
GENIE (*giving the jar to Zametti*): Then, take this accursed vessel. I must obey you. But know that your happiness is now gone and will never return. You will not see me again. Adieu!

(*More thunder and lightning. The Genie vanishes in the midst of a burst of flames. At this moment, Pietro regains control of his senses. He sees the Black Sarcophagus, still lit by livid illuminations, utters a scream of fear and flees. Zametti, holding the mysterious jar, steps forward, seized at the same time by a strange joy and a profound horror.*)

CURTAIN

Scene II

We are now in a great hall in Zametti's castle. At the back, there is a large stairway leading to Zametti's sanctum. (Light can be seen shining through the glass windows of the sanctum upstairs.). To the right and left, there are other doors, leading to various apartments. In the foreground, there is a table and several armchairs.

Cecilia enters from the left; young Antonio, Zametti's son, is asleep in an armchair.

CECILIA: I just saw my brother, my unfortunate brother. He told me he knows a way of bringing peace to Zametti's soul. May he succeed, and may my father give him the forgiveness he craves! (*casting her eyes on Antonio*) My little Antonio is still asleep. Let nothing disturb his rest! If he saw me so uneasy over his father's absence, he would want to ease my worries–dear child! Soon, you'll be able to call me your mother–how sweet it'll be for me to fulfill that duty!

(*Antonio's sleep suddenly seems troubled by a powerful nightmare.*)

CECILIA: But, Great God, what's wrong with him? (*running to him*) What can be causing him such anguish? Antonio! Antonio!
ANTONIO (*awakening with a start, rising abruptly and uttering a cry*): Father! (*looking at Cecilia who takes him in her arms*) Ah! It's you, my good friend? Oh! I was really frightened!
CECILIA: What happened, dear boy?

ANTONIO: I had the most frightful dream!
CECILIA: A nightmare? What about?
ANTONIO: It will make you as afraid if I tell you...
CECILIA: Perhaps, but you must tell me.
ANTONIO: Well, it seemed we were in my father's laboratory where, as you know, neither you nor I nor anyone else, is permitted to enter. I was sitting on your knees, and you were hugging me hard, very hard, and my father was kissing me, too. Suddenly, a huge man entered. It was impossible to look at him without trembling with terror. He came towards us, took me in his arms and tried to kill me. You and my father came to my rescue, but he easily knocked you down. Then, he and my father went away. There's my dream. It was awful, wasn't it?
CECILIA (*upset, despite herself, by Antonio's tale*): Yes, yes–no doubt... (*forcing herself to smile*) But, my dear Antonio, it was only a dream.
ANTONIO: Oh, to be sure I don't believe it. Besides, who would want to do me harm?
CECILIA (*embracing him*): Dear child!

(*Olben enters.*)

CECILIA: Ah, here's my father.

(*She goes to him and guides his steps.*)

ANTONIO: My old friend!
OLBEN (*embracing Antonio*): Hello, hello, child. (*to Cecilia*) Well, daughter, has Zametti returned yet?
CECILIA (*with a sigh*): No, not yet.
OLBEN: Night's coming on. It's time to go back to our cottage.

CECILIA: Oh, father, let's wait a little longer.
ANTONIO: Yes, yet for a little while.
OLBEN: We shall do so. But Zametti's delay worries me. What is he doing? What can be keeping him at this hour? Alas! For some time now, his studies have changed him! He's only rarely with us, and when you say something to him, he hardly replies–he, who used to be so cheerful, so likable!
CECILIA: His labors are absorbing him completely; you must excuse–
OLBEN: No question, and it's because I love him greatly that I feel sorry for his newfound condition. His wealth which, if I believe the gossip, is spread throughout the region, had nothing to do with my agreeing to your wedding. His virtues alone have made me consent.
CECILIA: He'll be the best and most tender of sons for you.
OLBEN: He will console me for the other son I lost and whose memory I ought to hate.
CECILIA: O father, Janskin loved you so much, too.
OLBEN: He caused my ruin.
CECILIA: If he were to present himself before you, could your arms remain closed to him?
OLBEN: If he presented himself–but that's impossible. (*knocking at the side door*) Someone's knocking.
CECILIA: Perhaps it's Zametti?
ANTONIO: Oh! Yes, yes–it must be my father.

(*He follows Cecilia who goes to open the door. Janskin appears.*)

ANTONIO (*uttering a cry of terror at the sight of Janskin*): Ah!
CECILIA (*in a low voice*): Janskin.

JANSKIN (*noticing Olben*): Oh God! My father!

(*He wants to rush to the old man but Cecilia stops him.*)

OLBEN: Who's there then? Antonio appears afraid.
CECILIA (*gesturing to Antonio to be quiet*): Father, it's not a stranger; it's a person attached to the castle.
OLBEN: Ah, fine.

(*He sits down and takes Antonio in his arms–the boy has gone to him after having understood from Cecilia that he's not to reveal anything.*)

CECILIA (*in a low excited voice to Janskin*): What are you doing here?
JANSKIN (*low to Cecilia*): I wanted to speak to you and calm your fears. I've seen Zametti. Thanks to my advice and my prayers, he won't–or at least, I hope so–execute a plan, the nature of which I cannot reveal to you. But tomorrow, let him lead you to the altar. Another, perhaps, and it will be too late.
CECILIA: How mysterious!
JANSKIN: I can't tell you more at this moment. My people are waiting for me–once again, dangers threaten them. Tomorrow, at daybreak, meet me at the Black Stone. I will see you there. Goodbye. Ah! How I would dearly love to kiss my father's hand before leaving!
OLBEN: Well, Cecilia, is he finally bringing reassuring news?
CECILIA (*gesturing to Janskin to approach him*): Yes, father, you can relax.

(*She takes her father's hand, which Janskin leans over and kisses tenderly.*)

OLBEN: Dear child, you still seem very emotional; I thought I felt a tear on my hand.

(*Janskin rises and makes a gesture of sorrow and tenderness. Dragged away by his sister, he's about to leave when, suddenly, there is a great uproar. Pietro enters. Janskin rapidly passes in front of him and disappears.*)

PIETRO: The Devil! Wasn't that the leader of–?
CECILIA (*excitedly and low to Pietro*): Silence!
PIETRO (*to himself*): Always the same thing! Everyone's always telling me to shut up!
OLBEN: Is that you, Pietro?
PIETRO: Yes, Master Olben, it's me.
CECILIA: Where did you leave your master?
PIETRO: In the forest.
CECILIA: In the forest!
PIETRO: Yes, and my word, were I to be mercilessly beaten, I would have to tell you the most terrible adventure ever to terrify an honest man. After having walked I don't know how many leagues in that evil forest, which is an abode for all the magicians and sorcerers in the land, we finally arrived in a place where it was impossible to see clearly, even in broad daylight...

(*At this moment Zametti enters, enfolded in a cloak, pale, with disorderly hair. Four servants carrying torches enter with him.*)

PIETRO (*continuing his tale*): Suddenly I saw, just as I see you–
ZAMETTI (*in a threatening voice*): Shut up!

PIETRO (*finally noticing his master*): Ah, mercy! (*to Zametti*) I'm shutting up, sir, I'm shutting up.
CECILIA (*going to Zametti*): At last, you're here, my friend!
ZAMETTI: Father!
OLBEN: Dearest Zametti, you really made us wait.
ZAMETTI (*after having kissed his son*): Pardon, pardon, father–and you, my Cecilia–important business has kept me much longer than I thought. I am in despair.
OLBEN: Well, here you are now, and all is forgotten. But mercy, take better care of your health and don't worry your friends like this any more. (*in a low voice*) You know, rumors are spreading about your mysterious labors... and why I granted you my daughter's hand... Destroy the instruments of your accursed science, Zametti, and then I will no longer worry about your future. We were all waiting for you. Is tomorrow, as we agreed, still the day when I call you my son?
ZAMETTI (*very excitedly and grasping Cecilia's hand*): Yes, yes, tomorrow, tomorrow.
OLBEN: The ceremony will take place in my home; that is something that was decided earlier. You will marry my Cecilia under a thatched roof and therefore you will never forget that you loved her for herself, not any worldly wealth. Goodbye, my friend. You know how dear you are to me. Your generous kindness has supported my old age, but I'll owe you even more still–my daughter's happiness. Think, I beseech you, that this other matter be completely put to rest by then. My little Antonio is going to come with me now, right?
ANTONIO: Very willingly.
CECILIA: Father, I'll be right behind you.
OLBEN (*pressing Zametti's hand*): Goodbye, goodbye.

(*Zametti embraces his child. Olben, Antonio, Pietro and the two servants leave.*)

CECILIA: One last word, my friend, and then I'll leave you alone.
ZAMETTI: What do you want, dearest Cecilia?
CECILIA: Did you see my brother?
ZAMETTI (*disturbed*): What! How?...
CECILIA: He told me, but fear not. He didn't confide your secrets to me. Today, I still want to respect them. (*smiling*) But tomorrow, don't forget that you must no longer keep any secrets from your wife.
ZAMETTI: Oh, believe that only the strongest necessity–
CECILIA: Shh. I'm not asking anything of you now. I don't want you to give me the least explanation about your evening. But take my father's advice: rest now. Your features are drawn, marked by too many sleepless nights. O my friend, from now on, let us be the only and sweetest subject of study for each other.
ZAMETTI: Dearest Cecilia.
CECILIA: Think carefully–if all my love and my efforts cannot dissipate the profound sadness and dark melancholy that, even now, I see on your face, then I can't but think that you no longer love me. That thought will poison my life and, soon, dearest Zametti, you will have lost your Cecilia.
ZAMETTI: What are you saying? Ah, I'd rather die a thousand times than cause you pain but for a moment! You ask that I abandon my labors? Very well, I intend to obey. Starting from tomorrow, this laboratory will be shut forever. I will deliver myself entirely to you, my Cecilia. I will be the happy possession of an adored ob-

ject, and no other thought, no matter how foreign, shall come to distract me from my love.
CECILIA: You are making a promise. I ought to... I want to believe it. I'll now catch up with my father. (*smiling and giving him her hand*) Goodbye, my dearest friend, goodbye.
ZAMETTI (*kissing Cecilia's hand*): Tomorrow I will start a new life.
CECILIA: Remember your oath. Goodbye!

(*She leaves with two other servants. Zametti, who watches her longingly as she departs, follows her to the door. Then, alone, he slowly walks towards the audience. Night has fallen. The stage is not lit, except for a lamp placed on the table in the foreground. Music depicting a storm rises*.)

ZAMETTI (*alone*): Yes, I swore an oath–but for tomorrow, tomorrow. Tonight remains mine. Must I leave such an enterprise incomplete? After so many years of work–the master of such an extraordinary power... Will I see it, then, destroyed without being able to hold its fruits in my hands? (*pointing to the laboratory*) The object of my experiment is there. If I were to succeed... (*taking a step, then stopping*) But all their ominous warnings dismay me! Perhaps another power, jealous of my triumph, seeks to thwart me by sowing doubts and fears? That is possible... (*rain and thunder*) What a dreadful night! The whistling of the wind is mixing with the rolls of thunder and the rain is falling in torrents. Such a project as mine demands such a night, however... (*taking the lamp*) Maybe one last try, then–but no imprudence! No presumptuous act! (*stopping after a moment of silence*) Yes–let's go!

(*He climbs the stairway and enters the laboratory. Meanwhile, Pietro enters by a side door carrying a lantern.*)

PIETRO (*as he enters*): My master has gone. I bet that he is in his laboratory, in the midst of his crucibles, his alembics and his whole arsenal of devilish crockery. Yet, he must get up early. Miss Cecilia has asked me to make sure of it. (*he bumps into a chair and drops his lantern, which goes out*) My God! Here I am, alone, in the dark! What's going to become of me?

(*Suddenly, a bluish flame appears in one of the laboratory windows.*)

PIETRO (*curious*): Heavens! What's that? I'm burning to find out. I've never felt so filled with courage–that's a good sign. Let's go closer.

(*He climbs and looks through one of the glass windows. A sudden explosion can be heard. The blue flame becomes red.*)

ZAMETTI (*from inside the laboratory*): What have I done? What have I done?

PIETRO (*rushing down the stairs shaking like a leaf*): What did I see? What did I see? (*falling to the ground*) O woe! Misfortune! I'm done for! (*rising and scrambling away on all fours*) I'm dead! Help! Help!

(*Zametti emerges from the laboratory, locks the door in terror and hurries down the stairs.*)

ZAMETTI: What Monster from Hell have I created? He breathed. His gaze was fixed on me! O Heaven! What work have I accomplished? What an object of horror! And it's to arrive at this fatal result that I have deprived myself of rest? A frightful light is now penetrating my very soul. Already my punishment begins, already everything tells me that I have deserved Heaven's justice. (*listening*) Everything is quiet now... Perhaps, the Monster has returned to nothingness... If only it were possible! Oh, no mortal could endure his presence–and I–wretch that I am–Olben, my son, my dearest Cecilia–I will no longer dare approach you. I am lost, lost forever.

(*He falls, overwhelmed, into a chair. Suddenly, the door of the laboratory begins creaking loudly, being slowly forced open by the Monster. Then, the locks break. The door, torn from its hinges, smashes into the bannister, breaks it and falls down to the stage.*

The Monster, wrapped in a huge cloak, appears on the threshold of the laboratory, framed by red flames. He rushes on stage, goes to Zametti and puts his huge hand on him.)

ZAMETTI (*rising, shocked*): Great God! It's him! I'm doomed!

(*The Monster looks attentively at Zametti, steps back, then for a second time approaches his creator, who recoils before him.*)

ZAMETTI: Monster, do not come near me! Withdraw or fear my wrath! No, no. What am I saying! You must not, cannot leave here...

(Zametti draws his sword and seeks to kill the Monster. But the Creature easily snatches the blade from his hands, breaks it and disappears into an abyss of darkness which opens suddenly.)

CURTAIN

Act II

Scene III

Another part of the same forest already seen in Act I. A rock to the right in the background. AT RISE, Janskin is seated on the side of the stage. Gypsies are arranged around a large fire over which a cauldron is suspended. Some are asleep. Others gamble and drink. The stage is half-obscure.

JANSKIN (*to himself*): Cecilia can't be late coming. Only a few more hours and–dare I hope?–my father's curse will no longer weigh on me. My father! Yesterday evening, he didn't suspect that it was the hand of his own son which so tenderly clasped his. Oh! I would have given my very life to press him to my heart. But that moment is merely deferred. As to Zametti–if he were to have accomplished his dreadful project, then, all hope would be lost. Fortunately, my friendship prevented his audacity–he gave me his word. He's marrying my sister today and this marriage will preserve him from all the dangers that his fatal ambition would otherwise expose him to.

(*Petrusco enters, running.*)

PETRUSCO: At last I'm back. (*giving a letter to Janskin*) Here, this is a letter that a villager gave me for you.
JANSKIN (*taking the letter and reading*): "I won't be able to come to our meeting because I can't leave our father, but I spoke to him. I've already sounded his heart

and everything gives me hope that this very day, he will pronounce your pardon." *(clasping the letter to his breast)* Oh, joy! Oh, happiness! (*to Petrusco*) Well, what else do have we to worry about?
PETRUSCO: Nothing. The Police, deceived by my clever tricks, have been misled into looking for us elsewhere. Besides, I left two of our men at the entrance to the forest. If they return, they'll warn us in time.
JANSKIN: So then, we can, without danger, remain camped in this part of the forest. (*to the Gypsies*) But our supplies are running low. Go get more and return promptly. (*to Petrusco*) They'll spend the rest of the day celebrating.
PETRUSCO: Yes, yes, it's agreed. Now, let's depart, hurry up! (*there's some movement to leave, but suddenly, at Petrusco's voice, everyone stops*) Silence! Someone's running from that side.
JANSKIN: Can it be one of our men? Coming to warn us that the Police–
PETRUSCO: No, it's one of the villagers.
JANSKIN: I recognize him now. It's Zametti's servant. He seems terrified. What does it mean?

(*Pietro enters and crosses the stage running, often looking behind him–as if someone was pursuing him–and not noticing the Gypsies.*)

PETRUSCO (*barring his way*): Stop!

(*The Gypsies surround Pietro.*)

PIETRO (*stopping, terrified*): Ah, good God! A den of thieves! I'm done for! Mercy, mercy!
GYPSIES (*angry*): He called us thieves!

PETRUSCO: We're Gypsies, do you understand?
PIETRO (*trembling*): Yes, yes, brave and honest Gypsies, if there ever were any, and I'm quite sure you wouldn't want to do any harm to a poor devil such as I.
JANSKIN (*whom Pietro has not yet seen*): Come closer and fear nothing.
PIETRO (*aside*): Him again! Decidedly, I meet him everywhere I go.
JANSKIN: Come closer, I tell you.
PIETRO: Yes, yes, sir! I'm coming closer. Here I am.
JANSKIN: Answer. Where were you going?
PIETRO: To Old Man Olben's cottage. He's a blind old man who dwells–
JANSKIN: I know him–and where are you coming from?
PIETRO: From my master's castle.
JANSKIN: Why this precipitous rush? You seemed terrified–what harm–
PIETRO: Oh! There are plenty of reasons, I assure you. If you knew what happened last night at the Castle, especially what I saw...
JANSKIN (*aside*): Great God! Could Zametti have forgotten his oath? (*aloud to the Gypsies*) Go, my friends! Leave here at once!
PIETRO: Can I leave too, excellent sir?
JANSKIN: No, you stay.
PIETRO: But–
JANSKIN: Stay, I tell you. I want to speak to you.
PIETRO: I want to speak to you–after we're alone.

(*The Gypsies leave. Pietro and Janskin remain alone.*)

JANSKIN: Now tell me, when I left Zametti last night, near the sarcophagus in the forest, did he go away immediately?
PIETRO: No, he stayed.
JANSKIN: And what did he do?
PIETRO: Upon my word, I can't tell you precisely because my master cast a spell on me. He did it like this–(*gesturing*) and I stayed so–
JANSKIN (*aside*): The wretch! Ah! I tremble–if he was able to obtain... (*aloud*) But what took place at his castle that was so frightening? What did you see?
PIETRO: Damnation! I saw–I can't very well tell you what I saw, because when you're afraid, you can't see. All that I can tell you is that I thought I saw *something* in my master's laboratory–something horrible–it was a face, a body, a Monster... No offense intended, but there are some in your tribe–with all due respect–that are not among the handsomest of men, you will agree. And yet, I've never seen anything as ugly as that creature.
JANSKIN (*aside*): No more doubt! The wretch has ruined himself–and my sister, and my father, too! Oh! May God at least give me the strength to help them and rescue them from the dreadful shadow that Zametti has now cast upon them all.
PIETRO: Is that all that you wanted to know? Can I now–
JANSKIN: Yes, you may go now, but say nothing of this to anyone, especially not to Cecilia–for if you were to speak...
PIETRO: I understand, sir, and since I now have your permision... (*bows and moves away, but then stops and looks in the direction from which he came*)
JANSKIN (*noticing Pietro's behavior*): Well? What are you waiting for?

PIETRO: Beg your pardon, sir, but I think I hear my master.
JANSKIN: Your master?
PIETRO: Yes, it's him. He's running this way. Like me–fear has given him wings.
JANSKIN (*aside, watching too*): The wretch! In what disorder–in what distraction–ah, no doubt about it, his punishment is beginning. (*to Pietro who keeps looking at him*) Go away!
PIETRO: Yes, yes, sir. (*aside*) Let's go quickly and look for the wedding party.

(*Pietro leaves from the right. Zametti, clothes and hair in disorder, enters from the left.*)

ZAMETTI: Go away, go away! Don't come near me, living spectre! What do you want with me? Why are you attaching myself to my very steps? Am I then prey that you intend to devour? Yes, it's I who called you into this world–that crime is indeed my work, and it's for you to punish me for it. Come drag me into the hell I pulled you from–but at least, let me be your only victim.
JANSKIN (*aside*): The unfortunate wretch! He's gone raving mad! (*goes to Zametti*) Zametti!
ZAMETTI: Who calls me?
JANSKIN: It is I, Janskin, your friend.
ZAMETTI: Janskin! Don't come near me. You would become the accomplice of my crime. You would become like me–a horror to the Earth, cursed by Heaven, exposed to all the tortures of Hell.
JANSKIN: Calm yourself, Zametti. Despite your crime, I feel only pity–
ZAMETTI: Pity for me! I don't deserve any! Did I myself show pity for my fellow men, when I cast upon the

Earth my execrable enemy? No, Heaven is just. Since the fatal moment when I dared to cross the bounds it imposes on humanity, its wrath has descended upon me.
JANSKIN: True, your crime is a monstrous one, Zametti, but the divine power of mercy is infinite too. Perhaps it has already made the Monster which you called to Earth with your presumptuous ambition return to nothingness.
ZAMETTI: No, no–during that night–that terrible night which saw me frozen in terror–then, I looked upon his face, the Monster's face!–he fled–but his frightful image still pursues me everywhere, haunts me, terrifies me. I've left my castle, exhausted, haggard. I nearly succumbed at the entrance to the forest, but I can find no rest, no peace. I'm still shivering. I noticed that the Monster seemed to enjoy my fear–one might have said that the Genie of that accursed tomb was smiling at his work of destruction.
JANSKIN: Calm down, Zametti. Perhaps your imagination has surrounded you with these dreadful illusions. Look around. Everything is calm here.
ZAMETTI: Yes, for the moment, but soon... (*listening and turning with terror*) Don't you hear? I think I see–
JANSKIN: Nothing! Come, banish these idle frights and hear the language of reason, and friendship.
ZAMETTI: Friendship! Do you dare to preserve yours for me?
JANSKIN: I wanted your happiness and that hasn't changed.
ZAMETTI: There is no more happiness for me. Everything is over. Death, death alone that I am calling, can put an end to the frightful torments that are devouring me.

JANSKIN: What are you saying? Didn't you have the courage to do evil? Are you without strength to repair it? You want to die! I think that Cecilia cannot survive your loss. And what about your son–will you leave him without support on Earth?
ZAMETTI (*returning little by little to himself*): Yes, my son, Cecilia, cherished objects, I have ruined you, ruined you forever.
JANSKIN (*in a solemn tone*): Listen: Fate ordained what took place. Cecilia's virtues ought to have kept you from the abyss. Now, these same virtues can still help you defeat Fate. Yes, I dare conceive hope. If you marry my sister, her candor, her innocence, her prayers will disarm the celestial wrath, and you can still hope for happy days.
ZAMETTI: Dear Janskin! What consoling hope you are causing to shine before my eyes.

(*Gypsy music is heard.*)

JANSKIN: My men are returning. They will enjoy their festivities now. You must go to my father's cottage. Prepare to lead Cecilia to the altar. I will soon join you there. Come with me, I'll take you to the edge of the forest.

(*They leave. Suddenly, the Monster appears on the rocks. As he descends, he expresses in pantomime the effect the light and the air is producing on him.*

He notices the fire, which excites his admiration. He seeks to take a piece of lighted wood from the furnace, but quickly stung by the fire, he withdraws his hand and expresses pain.

He hears the Gypsy music and listens in ecstacy. Diverse sensations are produced on him by the music. Upon the arrival of the Gypsies, he quickly withdraws.)

PETRUSCO (*to the Gypsies*): Come, my friends, while we await the return of our leader, let us dance and play games.

BALLET

(*Suddenly, the Monster reappears from behind the rocks. Everyone is shocked and terrified. There is much screaming and shouting. The Gypsies all escape and vanish.*)

CURTAIN

Scene IV

The stage represents Cecilia's room in Olben's cottage, and is open at the back. Far to the rear, we can see a small stream, crossed by a rustic bridge. Further back, there are mountains. On the one side, there is a door; on the other, a window.

Three villagers are helping Cecilia to finish dressing. She is looking at herself in a floor mirror. Little Antonio, Zametti's son, is there as well. Zametti's servants are bringing presents to the intended bride. It is a very animated tableau.

CECILIA: Here I am, ready at last. Thank you, thank you, my kind friends.
ANTONIO: Well, Cecilia, are you happy with your dress?
CECILIA: Yes, Antonio. Now your father can come when he pleases.
ANTONIO: How pretty you are with all this finery. But, come here, see what pretty things–
CECILIA: Yes, yes indeed. It's all much too beautiful for me. (*aside*) I hope Zametti has kept his promise...
ANTONIO: Nothing is too beautiful for you. (*to the villagers*) Let everybody know, do you hear? The wedding will take place at four!
VILLAGE GIRL: Don't worry, Master Antonio. There's no one in the village who isn't eager to witness our Mistress Cecilia's happiness.
CECILIA: Antonio, where is Olben?
ANTONIO: He went ahead to look for my father.

CECILIA: Zametti is late again... (*aside*) My God, I can't help but worry. (*suddenly a commotion is heard*) But what's that uproar? Here's Pietro. Perhaps he will tell us.

(*Pietro enters.*)

CECILIA: Good Pietro, what is the cause of this tumult?
PIETRO: It's those damned Gypsies again, Miss Cecilia.
CECILIA: Are they after someone? Should we–
PIETRO: No, quite to the contrary, Miss. It's they who are being pursued. One doesn't know by what or who, but they're running–running. I have good legs, too, when I'm scared, but I don't have speed like that!
ANTONIO: My father hasn't got here. I'll go ahead and wait for him at the end of the road.
CECILIA: Should you–
ANTONIO: Yes, yes! I can't wait to see him. Goodbye, Cecilia. (*to the villagers*) Come with me! (*to Cecilia*) I hope to soon bring back my father–your husband.

(*They go out.*)

PIETRO (*to himself*): Her husband! Ah, believe that if you will! I don't think there's much chance of this marriage taking place now.
CECILIA: Pietro, what are you saying there, all alone?
PIETRO: Nothing, Miss, absolutely nothing. I beg you even to notice that I've said nothing at all to you.
CECILIA: Really? And why's that?
PIETRO: You will remember, won't you, Miss? So that if the occasion demands it, I can call you as a witness.

CECILIA: Do you know, indeed, Pietro, that since you've arrived, I find you cloaked in an air of secrets and mystery.
PIETRO: That's true, Miss, but that's because I have my reasons.
CECILIA: And what are they?
PIETRO: Beg your pardon, Miss, but I have reasons for not tell you my reasons.
CECILIA: Come on, Pietro, there are secrets between–
PIETRO: Yes, there are, and big ones too, but please, Miss–I entreat you, don't make me blab. I really want to–it's my nature–but if I do, it'll be terribly unfortunate and, you see, it could compromise me.
CECILIA: Well then, I won't be indiscreet. Tell me, have you made all the preparations for the garden party? Everything is set up?
PIETRO: Yes, yes, Miss. The tables, the wine, the orchestra, everything is ready. All we need now are dancers, drinkers and musicians.
CECILIA: I hope our friends aren't late.

(*Some villagers are now coming and going outside, at the back of the stage.*)

PIETRO: No, Miss. Here they are.
CECILIA: Good! Take them to the garden. I will join you shortly.

(*Pietro goes to join the villagers. Cecilia returns to the back of the room.*

Suddenly, outside, we see the Monster skulking. He notices Cecilia in her room through the window. Her sight makes the greatest impression on him. He follows her with his eyes, ravished, as she putters about. He half-opens the door and looks at her with intoxication. His eyes fall on the floor mirror. He recoils at seeing his image, comparing his ugliness to Cecilia's beauty. He is so affected that he would smash the mirror which has revealed his misfortune to him, but suddenly he hears someone coming and quickly withdraws.

Janskin enters.)

JANSKIN (*aside*): Zametti's Creature is nowhere to be found. I marshalled my men but no one could find him. May God have driven him far from these parts, so that he doesn't bring terror and death amongst us. Another hour and if there's still no trace of him, Zametti will be married to my sister, and then we will be able to face whatever sinister fate threatens.
CECILIA (*turning ariound and noticing Janskin*): My brother!
JANSKIN: Dear Cecilia! Tell me, has Zametti arrived?
CECILIA: No, not yet; but surely he can't delay–
JANSKIN (*aside*): He ought to be here already! I don't like this at all!
CECILIA: What's the matter with you, my brother? You seem uneasy. I guess you fear that my father may resist our prayers? But surely, you've received my letter. I told you, everything makes me hope that we will succeed.
JANSKIN: Sweet Cecilia. My welfare is the sole care that occupies you. Ah! May you yourself soon be happy.
CECILIA: If you obtain your pardon, what else would there be for me to wish for? I will soon be joined with the one I love. You will come and stay near us. And my father will at last enjoy a peaceful life, surrounded by his loving children.

JANSKIN: May Heaven not let anything destroy such a sweet prayer.

(*We hear Antonio's voice in the distance.*)

ANTONIO (*outside*): Here he is! Here is my father!
CECILIA (*joyfully*): Zametti! My beloved!
JANSKIN: It is him! Soon, we will no longer have anything to fear.
CECILIA: Yes, yes, very soon. Reassure yourself, my brother.
JANSKIN (*crossing the stage*): My father! Ah! here's the moment so long awaited.

(*Olben enters, supported by Antonio and Zametti. The alchemist embraces Cecilia, expressing his joy at seeing her again. He also gives Janskin a knowing signal. The blind old man is, of course, unaware of Janskin's presence.*)

OLBEN: My children! Until now, I only had one to support me; soon, I shall have two.
JANSKIN (*low to Zametti*): You didn't notice–
ZAMETTI: No. I'm beginning to hope.

(*Antonio leaves and goes to play outside, at the back of the stage.*)

CECILIA (*to her father, after gesturing to Janskin and Zametti*): Father, there's a person here asking for you.
OLBEN: Me? What does he want?
CECILIA: He's come to bring you news of someone who was once very dear to you...

OLBEN: What are you talking about, child? Who may that be?
CECILIA: Your own son, father. He has come to speak to you about Janskin.
OLBEN (*with a gesture of joy that he attempts to suppress*): Janskin! My son! He still lives! But what does he wish to tell me? Cecilia, who is that man?
JANSKIN (*approaching*): Here I am, sir.
OLBEN: Is it my son who has sent you?
JANSKIN: Yes... yes.
OLBEN: What does he want then? What has become of his pride? You knew him, Zametti? Like you, he was smitten with an art which deserves only the wrath of Heaven and the scorn of men. He distanced himself from everything honorable, and rejected my advice and my entreaties. He caused my ruin, soiled my name and delivered me, like himself, to the horror of my fellow citizens, forcing me to an exile without return. Ah, I owe all the misfortunes of my life to him. After a silence of six years, what reason has he now to remember his father?
JANSKIN (*forcefully*): Ah! Never–trust my words–never has he forgotten you, nor has he ever ceased to cherish you.
OLBEN (*surprised, with a hint of recognition*): That voice!
JANSKIN: Yes, he has been guilty of many sins towards you, but if you only knew by how many hardships he's endured to expiate those sins! By all that's holy, don't shut him from your heart now. If you do not reject his solemn plea, all his life will henceforth be dedicated to you, to repair the wrongs he has caused.
OLBEN: You! You are–

JANSKIN (*falling to his feet*): Yes, yes, father, it is I, Janskin, your son, your unfortunate son who is coming to implore his pardon or die at your feet!
OLBEN (*pushing him away, feebly*): Great God! No– don't come near me. I can't–
CECILIA: Father, will you be merciless?
ZAMETTI: Won't you forgive him? In the name of Heaven, father, don't reject him.
OLBEN (*emotionally*): Cecilia, you have deceived me. I had sworn to be inflexible, but now that he is here, I have not the strength to resist. I can do nothing but open my arms to him.
JANSKIN (*throwing himself in his father's arms*): Father!
OLBEN: Cruel child. It's six years you've deprived me of this happiness.

(*Janskin and Cecilia are in Olben's arms.*)

ZAMETTI (*considering this picture of happiness*): O all-merciful God, I render you thanks–watch over them, and if you must, take me and me alone for your victim.

(*At the back of the stage, the Monster suddenly appears on the bridge. Antonio, seeing him, lets out a frightful shriek. Everybody turns and runs toward the child. But as this action takes place, the Monster has already vanished.*)

CECILIA (*running to Antonio and supporting him in his arms*): Antonio, great God. What is it?
ZAMETTI: My son!
OLBEN: What's wrong with him?
JANSKIN: Why this scream of terror?

(*Pietro returns.*)

PIETRO: Hey, what's happened to him?
ANTONIO (*still in shock, to Cecilia*): Ah! If you knew...
CECILIA: What?
ZAMETTI: Speak, speak, my son.
ANTONIO (*still to Cecilia, who holds him in her arms*): You remember that terrifying face that I was telling you about this morning and that I saw in my dream?
CECILIA: Well?
ANTONIO: Just now, as I was playing back there, I saw it. Him.
ALL: Where?
ANTONIO (*pointing to the bridge*): There! There!
ZAMETTI (*aside, in extreme terror*): O terror! He saw *him*!
JANSKIN (*aside*): Could *he* have come here? (*hurriedly, to the villagers*) Come, my friends, come! Let's find out what frightened our little Antonio so much.

(*Janskin, leading the villagers, rush out of the rear. Meanwhile, Pietro stands in one corner, while Zametti, Cecilia, still comforting Antonio, and Olben stand in another.*)

PIETRO (*aside*): See how they run! But not me! I'm not at all curious. I've already been taken once.
ZAMETTI (*aside*): My strength is abandoning me. O Heaven, are my frightful forebodings going to be fulfilled?
CECILIA (*aside, scutinizing Zametti*): What terror is depicted in his features.
OLBEN: Does some new misfortune threaten us again?

ZAMETTI (*excitedly seizing Olben's hand*): Oh no, no– fear not, father.
CECILIA (*aside, still looking at Zametti*): The worry that I read in his eyes scares me despite myself.
OLBEN (*to Zametti, in a low voice, clutching his hand*): Could you have reneged on your oath? Should I believe that, far from abandoning your culpable labors–
ZAMETTI (*in an altered voice*): No. Don't think that.
OLBEN: Still, your hand trembles in mine.

(*Zametti's disarray is now complete. He tries to distance himself from Olben–and to avoid Cecilia's scrutiny. Fortunately for him, Janskin returns with the mob of villagers.*)

JANSKIN: We didn't find anything.
ZAMETTI (*eyes ardently fixed on Janskin*): Nothing?
JANSKIN: No. (*with a forced smile*) Our little Antonio was letting his imagination run wild–no doubt.
ZAMETTI (*aside*): If only!
CECILIA: Yes, yes... that's probably the case...
ANTONIO: Oh! No, Cecilia, I really saw–

(*At this moment, the village clock strikes four. Pietro rejoins the little group.*)

PIETRO (*with joy*): Ah! At last, the bells are ringing! They're calling us.
OLBEN: It's the hour of the ceremony. Let's go.
CECILIA (*going excitedly to Zametti and taking his hand*): Father, you are going to bless our union.

(*General commotion. Young girls surround Cecilia, placing the marriage crown on her head. Cecilia and*

Zametti bow at Olben's feet as he blesses them. As this is happening, the Monster reappears on the bridge, then hides again. The music stops. Zametti and Cecilia rise.)

OLBEN: Give the final signal for departure. (*to the villagers*) Come, my friends!
PIETRO: Let's go. I will lead the way.

(*Pietro arranges the villagers in marching order. Antonio and Olben leave with them to the accompaniment of joyful music. Cecilia, who seems lost in her thoughts, goes to Zametti and stops him.*)

CECILIA: Before marching to the altar, I would speak with you for a moment.

(*Zametti and Janskin exchange a concerned look.*)

JANSKIN: Why?
ZAMETTI: Dear Cecilia, in the name of Heaven, let's not indulge in a moment's delay!
JANSKIN: Sister, I beseech you, come!
CECILIA (*looking from Zametti to Janskin*): No. This conversation is necessary.
JANSKIN: If you value your own happiness–
CECILIA: Yes, it's precisely in the name of that very happiness that I must have it.
JANSKIN (*carried away despite himself*): If only you knew–
CECILIA: Knew what?
ZAMETTI (*concerned*): Nothing, nothing, dearest Cecilia. I will talk to you. Please go away, Janskin. (*low and hurriedly to Janskin*) But stay near and keep an eye on us.

(*Janskin appears annoyed. As he steps aside, he expresses his fears and concern to Zametti with a gesture.*

Meanwhile, none of the characters have yet noticed the Monster in the background. When he saw the villagers head off towards the church, he came out from his hiding place. When he stares at Cecilia, his gestures and the looks on his face express the effect that the young girl's beauty has upon him.

Throughout, Zametti appears filled with unease and impatience, and frequently looks around him.)

CECILIA (*intently, to Zametti*): Now that we are alone, my beloved, I want to ask you something–and my entire, future happiness shall depend on your answers. Before we're joined in matrimony forever, you owe me the whole truth. I will not lie to you: the unease I saw painted on your face has pierced my soul like a dagger. A thousand suspicions are tearing my heart apart...
ZAMETTI: O Heaven! What do you mean? (*aside*) I am dying of fear.
CECILIA: Have you kept your promise? Today, no dark cloud should alter your features. Yesterday, you swore to abandon my labors and shut your laboratory forever. You said: "I will deliver myself entirely to you. I will be the happy possession of an adored object, and no other thought, no matter how foreign, shall come to distract me from my love." Your love! Ah! Should I still believe in it?
ZAMETTI: Ah! Cecilia, what word did you just pronounce? Me–to have ceased for even an instant to love you, to adore you!

CECILIA: Yet if you loved me, would you have hidden a single one of your thoughts? Or is it I and I alone who is the cause of your trouble? Have you come to regret your vows? To see poor Cecilia as unworthy indeed of aspiring to be your wife? If so, speak! There's still time.
ZAMETTI: Stop, Cecilia, I won't let you say another word of this. Great God! Are you taking pleasure in ripping my heart apart? What a time have you chosen to burden me with such unjust accusations. Ah! This last blow is all my misfortune needed! Cruel friend, you doubt my love when it's the last and only hope of happiness. Yes, I ought to reveal a terrible secret, which weighs dreadfully on my soul–but I swear in the face of that God who will soon receive our oaths that, far from breaking the binds that unite us, it will only tighten them further. By leading you to the altar, I am seeking to enlist your virtues–my fate depends on it.
CECILIA (*eyes fixed on Zametti's*): What strange talk! What does it mean?
ZAMETTI: Moments are precious. Come, come, my beloved.
CECILIA: I must trust your sincerity. Yes, you love me. To doubt it longer would only offend us both. Your fate depends on me, you say? Ah! Then, it's going to be a happy one, for I am with you. Let's rejoin my father.
ZAMETTI (*pressing Cecilia in his arms*): Darling Cecilia, mine–mine forever.

(*The Monster creeps closer to the two lovers. He admires Cecilia, devours her with his eyes. Seeing her in Zametti's arms, he is no longer able to control his passion. He rushes toward the young girl as she is about to head toward the church.*

Cecilia finally notices the Monster, who is extending his arms towards her. She utters a terrible scream and escapes toward the bridge.)

ZAMETTI: It's him. O despair!

(*The Monster seeks to pursue Cecilia, but Zametti blocks his way, standing in his path. The Monster knocks him over and runs towards the bridge where Cecilia stands, terrified.*)

ZAMETTI: Cecilia! Unfortunate Olben! I am unarmed!

(*He gets up. At this moment, some armed villagers appear at the back. Zametti grabs a musket from one of them and rushes after the Monster. Olben, too, arrives.*)

OLBEN: My daughter! My Cecilia!

(*At this moment, Cecilia's strength finally abandons her. She faints and falls into the Monster's arms. Surprisingly, he gently carries her and deposits her in Olben's arms, expressing his joy and no longer displaying the untamed passion he displayed earlier.*)

OLBEN (*recognizing Cecilia*): Cecilia! Cecilia! She doesn't respond to me.

(*Cecilia eventually comes to, notices the Monster, screams in terror and throws herself in the arms of her father.*

At this moment, Zametti arrives, armed with his musket. He aims at the Monster, fires and wounds him griev-

ously. The Creature utters a terrible howl, surrenders to his rage and, taking a flaming firebrand from the fire, sets fire to the cottage.

Soon, the flames are rushing in all directions. Vainly, Janskin and the villagers attempt to stop their furor but the conflagation soon spreads. Olben appears unable to escape the flames which now surround him.

Zametti manages to carry off Cecilia and Antonio as the cottage collapses.

In the back, the Monster applauds his triumph, pointing to his wound.)

CURTAIN

Act III

Scene V

The stage represents a plush salon. The back opens onto a balcony which gives on the sea. To the right and left are doors which give on other apartments.

AT RISE, Cecilia is still unconscious. Several villagers lavish help on her. Antonio is near her, weeping as he kisses one of her hands.

PIETRO: Poor young Miss Cecilia! In what a state she is! But it's not surprising after all that's happened to her. It's really done things to her mind.
ANTONIO (*to Cecilia*): My good friend, my good friend, will you answer me?
PIETRO (*aside*): I'm really afraid now that she will never respond.

(*Janskin enters precipitously.*)

JANSKIN: Well, my friends, how is she? What? She still hasn't regained her senses? Poor Cecilia! Will I then have your death to deplore? That of my father was not already a misfortune big enough?
ANTONIO (*with sudden joy*): Ah! My God. If I'm not mistaken, her hand just clasped mine.
JANSKIN (*coming closer*): Can it be possible?
PIETRO: Yes, yes, God be praised! She's coming to herself!

JANSKIN: Silence, my friends.
CECILIA (*coming to little by little*): Where am I? What frightful dream did I have? But how did it happen? This wedding dress... Antonio, my brother, my friends, in the name of Heaven, please dispel my terror! Why am I here? You don't say anything... Oh! I see it only too well... It was not a dream–and I no longer have a father.
JANSKIN: Courage, dear Cecilia. We all need strength to deal with this frightful blow.
CECILIA: So it really *is* true! My father! I will never see him again. (*she starts crying*)
ANTONIO: Come, my good friend, don't weep like that.
CECILIA: And Zametti, I don't see him. Why isn't he here with us?
JANSKIN: Perhaps he didn't dare appear before you. After all, isn't he the cause of all our ills? Wasn't he the one who brought us death and misfortune? Isn't he now and forever an object of abomination for the entire world?

(*Zametti enters through the back. Upon seeing him, the villagers move away, shocked.*)

VILLAGER: There comes the sorcerer! Let's get out of here!
ZAMETTI: You're right, Janskin.Your resentment is just. But soon, you will no longer have anything to fear. Soon, you will be delivered of my presence. Pietro!

(*But Pietro does not dare to step forward and approach his master.*)

ZAMETTI: Take them to the great hall of my castle. There, I will soon reveal my last intentions. And take Antonio with you.
ALL THE VILLAGERS (*muttering*): He should go away! Leave!

(*Amidst much grumbling, the villagers finally leave, followed by Pietro, holding Antonio's hand.*)

JANSKIN: Zametti, you see the hate and execration that your people feel for you. That's the price of your abominable conduct, the effects of your detestable, blind ambition.
ZAMETTI: Janskin, for pity's sake, don't berate me further. I know what wretched thing I did. Spare me your sermons.
JANSKIN: Spare you! Your crime has broken all the bonds that once existed between us. Don't hope that my sister or I will ever forgive you.
ZAMETTI: What say you, dear Cecilia? You, too, would be insensitive to the sorrows of the miserable creature that I am?
CECILIA: Ah, let me alone to weep for my father!
ZAMETTI: Poor Olben! Remember that I, too, cherished him. I, too, called him father. Heaven is my witness that I would instantly give my life to buy his back. I know full well that I am the cause of his death. I feel it in my soul. I realize that you can no longer look at me now, except with horror; but at least, leave me with the hope that, one day, I may be able to gain your forgiveness. It's the only consolation capable of supporting me through my misfortunes Cecilia, would you deprive me of that?

CECILIA: What are you asking that of me? Cruel man! Look at what you have done! I loved you with all my heart; my happiness was soon to be yours. Yet you allowed your folly to destroy such sweet hopes and turn a day of joy into a day of mourning and desolation.
ZAMETTI: Ah! Don't reproach my crime–Heaven has already too cruelly punished me. But I now stand ready to expiate my fault, to try to repair the wrongs I have caused. I'm going to leave you, Cecilia. I'll flee far from these parts. It's the only way to attract the danger to myself, and to preserve the beings who are dearest to me. Perhaps my repentance and my sufferings will succeed in appeasing the celestial wrath. Perhaps I will be permitted one day to return and implore my pardon at your feet.
JANSKIN: Wretch! How can you believe that your Monster won't reappear in these lands, returning to bring new misfortunes or seeking new victims?
ZAMETTI: No, Janskin. Wherever I am is where he directs his furor. Once I'm gone, the peril will all but disappear–for you. But before leaving, before saying one final goodbye, dear Cecilia, won't you allow yourself to feel some pity for me and grant some hope to the most unfortunate of men?
CECILIA: No! You gambled with my love, you asked Heaven–so you told me–only for the joy of being united to me forever, and yet another foul desire filled your heart. I was not what you held dearest and in listening to your mad ambition, you knowingly exposed us all to the worst dangers–and worse, even that knowledge proved incapable of stopping you! Cruel man, was it thus that you ought to have rewarded my love?
ZAMETTI: It's love itself that made me guilty, Cecilia. It was you alone who inspired my labors. You were ever

the sole object of all my thoughts. I wanted to raise you above all other mortals. I realize now my fatal error, and believe me when I say I have been well punished for it–and not by you. Cecilia, Janskin, look upon my tears, my despair. Am I then, for you too, an object of horror and fear?
JANSKIN (*moved despite himself, pressing Zametti in his arms*): I can no longer resist your cries of repentance. Sister, you cannot hate him. If we abandon him, who then will love him on Earth?
CECILIA (*abandoning her hand to Zametti*): Hate him! Alas! He knows too well what an empire he exercises over this heart that tore apart.
ZAMETTI (*transported with joy*): You do forgive me! I am still loved by you. I can now endure life.
JANSKIN: Zametti, I am again your devoted friend, your brother; but I insist you execute the plan you've devised. Leave this region for some time; it's necessary.
ZAMETTI: Of course! I shall depart this very night and not return until I am worthy of you.

(*Petrusco enters, running in some disarray.*)

PETRUSCO: Janskin! Janskin! The villagers told the Police that we're hiding in this castle with you. They're surrounding us on all sides. I refused to open the doors and let them in, and now they're threatening to lay siege to it. You're our only hope. What are we to do?
JANSKIN: Resist! Triumph–or die!
CECILIA: O my brother! I fear for you! Resistance is hopeless.
ZAMETTI: I will fight with you, Janskin. Swords in hand, we shall repel these odious mercenaries.

PETRUSCO: They're also prepared against you, Master Zametti. They know they owe the abomination which threatens them to you.
ZAMETTI: To me!
PETRUSCO: Yes. You've become the horror of these lands, the sorcerer whose criminal science has drawn the wrath of God upon our heads. They've brought torches and...
JANSKIN: Silence, my friend! These reproaches are useless now–it's a question of common security.
CECILIA: Misfortunes piled upon misfortunes!
ZAMETTI: Perhaps it is I alone whom they want? Well, I shall surrender to them and deliver you from the execrable author of your miseries!
JANSKIN: No, stay by my sister. Your duty is to protect her. She no longer has any support except you.
ZAMETTI: Alas!
CECILIA: Do as he asks!
ZAMETTI: It really is your wish, Cecilia? That is what you want? If so, yes, of course I will stay. I must watch over you... (*with an air of distraction*) Perhaps *he*, too, is watching over us–this enemy more dreadful by himself alone than all those who are now besieging us. Leave, Janskin, I will soon rejoin you. (*to Cecilia*) And you, my love, follow me. (*he escorts her to her apartment*)
CECILIA (*taking Zametti by one hand and Janskin by the other*): My fate is fixed. Don't forget–the moment of the death of either of you will be that of mine!
JANSKIN: Go! All is not yet lost. Goodbye, Zametti! I go to do battle.

(*Janskin draws his sword and leaves hurriedly with Petrusco right behind him.*

Zametti enters the apartment to the right with Cecilia. Hardly have they gone when the Monster appears. He points to his wound, expresses the pain it is causing him and silently swears to exact vengeance. Suddenly, he hears a noise. It is Antonio who is coming from the left with Pietro. Upon seeing the child, the Monster's face acquires an expression of infernal joy. He hides.)

PIETRO (*pulling Antonio after him and struggling with him*): I say that you will come with me.
ANTONIO: I want to go to my father.
PIETRO: It's your father himself who ordered you to be taken to the other wing of the castle where we will have much less danger to fear.
ANTONIO: Danger? My father and Cecilia are in danger then? Oh, in that case, I want even less to remain with you.
PIETRO (*in a tearful tone*): Antonio, in the name of Heaven, be reasonable and obedient. Don't cause pain to your poor friend Pietro. He's had quite enough of that already. And then it would also displease your father, who's my excellent and unfortunate master.
ANTONIO: Oh! I beg you, Pietro–allow me to see him and embrace him one more time.
PIETRO: God Almighty! How can anyone be as stubborn as this? You were entrusted to my protection and you will do as I say. If something bad happened to you, what would become of me?
ANTONIO (*struggling*): No! no! (*pointing to the door at the right*) My father is there with Cecilia. I want to stay ith them.
PIETRO: No! Come, come!
ANTONIO (*tearing himself from Pietro's hands and running towards the door*): No! Father! Father!

(*The Monster, who has been watching the scene attentively, suddenly grabs the child as he runs by him. He quickly puts his hand over Antonio's mouth and throws the boy over his shoulder. Pietro turns, sees him and utters a cry of pure terror.*).

PIETRO (*fleeing, in terror*): Help! Help! (*he runs away*)

(*Zametti emerges from Cecilia's room, pistol in hand.*)

ZAMETTI (*to Cecilia who cannot be seen*): Stay here, Cecilia! (*aside*) Whose scream did I hear? (*noticing the Monster*) It's him! O despair! My son!
ANTONIO (*screaming*): Father! Father!
ZAMETTI (*aiming his pistol at the Monster*): Halt, execrable creature!

(*He's about to shoot, but the Monster holds the boy in front of him, using him as a living shield to thwart the weapon threatening him. Zametti is forced to spare the Monster's life in order to save Antonio's.*)

ZAMETTI (*distraught, throws his pistol to the ground*): You win, you foulest of demons! You have nothing to fear from me–but return my son to me!

(*The Monster expresses his hate and his hope of vengeance.*)

ZAMETTI (*falling to his knees*): Yes, I have been cruel towards you. So avenge yourself on me. I offer myself to your blows–but not my son. Spare his life!

(Zametti, on his knees, implores the Monster's mercy. But instead, the Monster vanishes through the wall, taking the child with him. Zametti utters a harrowing scream.)

ZAMETTI: My son! He's taking my son with him! He's going to sacrifice him to his rage. My son! My dear child! So I, too, have become your murderer. (*he falls to the ground*)

(*Cecilia emerges from her room.*)

CECILIA (*addressing an unseen servant*): Let me go! I've heard horrible screams! I must see what happened to Zametti!

(Noticing the alchemist on the floor, she runs towards him and helps him back to his feet.)

CECILIA: Zametti! O merciful Heaven! What happened?
ZAMETTI (*looking at her but not seeing her really, so distraught he is*): What do you want of me? Flee! This is the abode of the Furies! Flee, I tell you, or you will be his prey, too!
CECILIA: He's going mad! In the name of Heaven, Zametti, tell me what happened!
ZAMETTI (*saner*): What do you want to know? That I am the most wretched of fathers? Well, yes. The same Heaven that I sought to appease has rejected my prayers. It has delivered the most defenseless among us to my horrible enemy. Hold! Can't you hear those screams? Those screams of agony? They are my son's!
CECILIA: O Heaven! Not Antonio?

ZAMETTI: Yes! He is no more!
CECILIA: O despair.

(*She falls into Zametti's arms. A horrible uproar is heard. Janskin, Pietro, Petrusco, some Gypsies and several servants rush in.*)

PIETRO (*entering first*): All is lost! All is lost!
JANSKIN (entering, sword in hand): We have lost! Most of my men have been taken prisoners or killed. Already the Police are masters of the first wall. In a moment, they will be here.
CECILIA: O my God! Protect us!
ZAMETTI: It's me they want. You have nothing to fear, Cecilia.
JANSKIN: It's over. Our fate has been accomplished. There's still hope however. One avenue of escape remains open to me–and my sister. A ship, manned by some of my best men, is moored outside this castle, ready to sail as soon as we're on board. But you, Zametti, recall your courage. It's now necessary for you to seek a noble death.
ZAMETTI: I agree and I'm ready.
CECILIA: No!
JANSKIN: He cannot escape his fate, Cecilia.
CECILIA: Why not?
JANSKIN: Zametti has been convicted of the darkest sorcery. The Council of Ten has sentenced him to death. Better an honorable death than the tortures of the Inquisition!
CECILIA: I shall die too!

(*Cecilia faints. Overwhelmed, Zametti remains silent. At the right of the stage, Janskin seizes the opportunity to pick up his sister. Aided by his followers, he takes her away and leaves by the left. There is some commotion in the background. Everybody else leaves in panic.*)

ZAMETTI (*alone*): Is Heaven–or Hell–satisfied? Am I sufficiently punished? What more do they want of me? God demanded my punishment. Is it sufficiently horrible? (*with a terrifying smile*) His envoy has fulfilled his mission! He's ravished everything from me–son, spouse, friends. I've lost everything. I remain alone in the world and yet, I still live, still foul this land with my odious presence! Goodbye, Cecilia. Goodbye, Janskin. Olben, Antonio, my son–it's I, I who've led you to the tomb–you will be avenged. The Council of Ten demands my head! But it's not on a pyre that I must end my life. My fate is inextricably linked to that of the execrable executioner of my loved ones. Come! Come! The Monster is calling for a final victim and I shall deliver him one!

(*Janskin returns with a few Gypsies.*)

JANSKIN: The Police have been momentarily driven back. For my sister's sake, I can't leave you behind. Come, wretch, I can still save you.
ZAMETTI: For Cecilia's sake...
JANSKIN: Yes. She's calling for you. She says she can't live without you. See the lightning, hear the drums of thunder–the storm is coming. It will protect our flight. Let's leave.

(*He drags him off. They leave by the right.*)

CURTAIN

Scene VI

The stage represents the exterior of Zametti's castle, located atop a cliff overlooking the Adriatic Sea.

Janskin's Gypsies, chased by the Police, rush onto the stage. A battle ensues between them and the Venetian soldiers. Finally, the Gypsies, defeated by the Police, are forced to flee.

CURTAIN

Scene VII

The stage represents the deck of Janskin's ship. It is buffeted by the waves, caught in a violent storm. The voices of sailors are mixed with the whistling of the wind and the claps of thunder. The greatest disorder reigns amongst the crew. Zametti, Janskin and Cecilia stand at center stage. Janskin is issuing instructions to his men.

JANSKIN: My friends, hold the sails. Petrusco, weigh anchor. Charge the depth.
GYPSY: Clear the topsail!
JANSKIN: Clear the topsail!
GYPSY: We're lost!
JANSKIN: No! Deploy the foresail! Haul up the big sail!

(*Suddenly, the Monster appears on a frail skiff. He seeks to board the ship. Cries of terror by all the crew.*)

GYPSIES: The Monster! The Demon! Help!

(*Despite the Gypsies' strong resistance, the Monster succeeds in hurling himself onto the deck. He pushes the men in his path as if they were cardboard cutouts. The remaining sailors flee in fear.*

The storm increases. Strange, eerie hapes appear amidst the waves: the Genie of the Sarcophagus? Avenging angles? Demons perhaps?

Finally, the Monster reaches Zametti. Cecila screams. The Alchemist remains motionless and does not try to flee.

Janskin tries to stop the creature but is swatted away. The Monster grabs Zametti, lifts him high above his head and hurls him into the raging sea.

Then, he raises his arms again and lets out a powerful scream of rage. Lightning strikes him down and he, too, falls into the sea.

The storm abates; the final tableau shows Janskin, holding Cecilia crying in his arms.)

CURTAIN

The Hunchback of Notre-Dame

by
Paul Foucher & Paul Meurice

based on the novel by
Victor Hugo

translated and adapted
by
Frank J. Morlock

Introduction

Notre-Dame de Paris (*The Hunchback of Notre-Dame*, 1831) was one of Victor Hugo's earliest and most popular novels. In it, he recaptured the ambience of Medieval Paris and introduced several unforgettable characters: Esmeralda, the doomed Gypsy girl with her fortune telling goat; Dom Claude Frollo, the pious monk who saved the deformed infant Quasimodo from death, only in later years to become the first stalker in literature, destroying Esmeralda, the girl he desires, and Quasimodo, whom he helped raise. In the end, Frollo becomes demented, and Quasimodo emerges as the inarticulate, but very real, hero of *Notre-Dame de Paris*.

The story was dramatized in 1850 by Paul Foucher and Paul Meurice. It is that version that we translated here.

Victor Hugo:

Victor Hugo (1802-1885) was born in Besançon in Eastern France. His father was a Bonapartist General, his mother a strong Monarchist. Young Hugo was something of a child prodigy, turning out translations of Latin and Greek when he was 13 and winning literary prizes when he was still in his teens. By the time he was 20, Hugo had already become not only a published poet, but one whom many regarded as France's greatest living poet. At 14, he is reputed to have said, "I want to be Chateaubriand or nothing." Three years later, Chateaubriand himself was calling Hugo an "enfant sublime." By 1823, he had already received Royal subsidies for his writings.

Hugo came to Paris and fell under the influence of Charles Nodier and the first Cenacle. With Alexandre Dumas, he became the leader of the Romantic Movement in the theater. In 1823 and 1824, he published two lurid, Gothic novels, *Han d'Islande* (*Han of Iceland*) and *Bug-Jargal* (1824). In 1827, he published his play, *Cromwell*, and the more influential, *Preface to Cromwell.* In it, he developed his theatrical ideas, which he derived in part from Shakespeare, advocating the mixing of the grotesque with the sublime. His next play, *Marion DeLorme*, based on the life of a famous 17th century courtesan, fell victim to censorship for political reasons.

In 1830, Hugo brought out *Hernani*, which was performed by the Comédie Française. Supported by his friends Dumas, Theophile Gautier, Alfred de Vigny and others, the first performance became a veritable battle between Hugo's friends and the outraged Classicists. The curious thing about the so-called "Battle of *Hernani*" was that, while the Romanticists tended to be politically sympathetic to Republicanism, the Republicans themselves tended to be very hostile to Romanticism in the theatre, and were actually strong supporters of Classicism. The reverse was the case with the Monarchists. Politically conservative, they were more open to theatrical innovation. But for the time being, for a period of about five years, the Romanticists were in the ascendant.

The next decade was the most prolific in Hugo's life. *Notre-Dame de Paris* (1831) made him immensely popular and, ultimately, got him a seat at the prestigious Académie Française in 1841. His dramatic successes included *Le Roi s'amuse* (*The King Amuses Himself*, 1832), adapted by Giuseppe Verdi for the opera *Rigoletto* (1851), the prose drama *Lucrèce Borgia* (1833) and the melodrama *Ruy Blas* (1838). However, in 1843, due to the twin blows of the failure of his latest play, *Les Burgraves*, and the drowning of one of his daughters and her husband, Hugo bid the theatre adieu.

Hugo's plays were not box office successes. He often envied Dumas who, though a lesser poet, enjoyed far greater popular success. The reason for his relative failure was, as an admirer, André Breton, observed, "taken as a whole the theatre of Hugo is monotonous and artificial." Honoré de Balzac, also an admirer and friend, remarked, "the characters are not created according to good sense." And after seeing *Les Burgraves*, "Victor Hugo has decidedly remained the "enfant sublime," and that's all he will ever be."

Hugo then decided to become more involved in politics. After escaping the early influence of his mother's Monarchism, he had became a lifelong Republican, even though he had been made a peer of France by King Louis Philippe in 1845. In particular, Hugo became a sworn enemy of Louis Napoleon, the future Emperor Napoleon III. His opposition to the coup d'état of 1852 eventually resulted in a 15-year-long exile to the Channel Islands of Jersey and Guernsey. It was there that he wrote his epic poem *La Légende des Siècles* (*The Legend of the Ages,* 1859-1883) and completed his longest and most famous novel, *Les Misérables* (1862).

After the fall of the Second Empire in 1870, Hugo returned to Mainland France and was elected to the National Assembly and, later, to the Senate. His latest works include the swashbuckling historical novel about the French Revolution, *Quatre-Vingt-Treize* (*Ninety-Three*, 1874) and a collection of beautiful poems about his grand-children entitled *L'Art d'être Grand-Père* (*The Art of Being a Grandfather*, 1877).

While Hugo will always be remembered as a novelist and poet, his contributions to the theatre, and especially the monumental adaptations of his novels, should not be neglected.

If Hugo may have been said to have had no sense of theatre when he wrote plays, the reverse was true when he wrote novels. These abound in vivid characters and scenes, which are both striking and seemingly real. When we come to the theatrical adaptations of his novels by Paul Foucher and Paul Meurice, we are presented with stunning plays that exhibit none of the faults usually associated with Hugo's original dramatic efforts.

Paul Foucher:

Foucher (1810-1875) was Hugo's brother-in-law. He attended the prestigious Lycée Henry IV in Paris with Alfred de Musset and the Duke of Orléans. From childhood, he was a friend of Victor Hugo and became his brother-in-law when Hugo married his sister in 1822.

Foucher was a sincere admirer of Hugo. When he was 19, Hugo, looking for easy money, had written a play, *Kenilworth*, based upon a Walter Scott novel, in collaboration with another dramatist, Alexandre Soumet (1786-1845). However, the two authors did not see eye to eye, Hugo favoring melodrama and Soumet comedy. Failing to reach an agreement, they each took the parts that they had written. Soumet went on to reuse his material to create *Emilia* which had a successful run at the Théâtre Français in 1827. For his part, Hugo produced his own play, which he entitled *Amy Robsart*, but never succeeded in getting it produced.

Six years later, in 1827, Foucher, by then the younger of Hugo's two brothers-in-law, begged him to let him read the shelved play (which had in fact, been recommended to him by Soumet himself!) with an eye to producing it himself. But Hugo was understandably reluctant to let what he considered to be an imperfect work written when he was 19 be exhumed. Foucher insisted and prevailed only by convincing Hugo to let *Amy Robsart* appear under Foucher's name, thus helping the latter's budding career. But Hugo was not the type of man to let things rest. He considerably rewrote the play.

Still, the rewritten *Amy Robsart*, which opened on February 13, 1828, at the Odéon, proved a total failure. Hugo, ever the honorable man, saved his brother-in-law from public humiliation by fessing up to it, writing to the newspapers: "*Since the success of* Amy Robsart, *the first essay of a young poet whose fortune is dearer to me than my own, has met with such bitter opposition, I hasten to declare that I am not altogether a stranger to the work. There are, in the drama, some passages, some fragments of scenes, which were written by me, and I ought to say that they are the passages which were, perhaps, most loudly hissed.*"

Whatever negative impression *Amy Robsart* might have left, it did not hurt Foucher's career. He earnestly began writing plays in 1830, and in 1832, novels as well. He was supposedly of a middling intelligence but those who wanted to get close to Hugo found it useful to be friends with him. Others fled this spoiled "child of romanticism" as he was called. His gaffes were legendary; at one time, calling Lamartine M. Prat. He was closely linked to Saint-Beuve who was an admirer (or lover) of Madame Hugo. Foucher's literary output was considerable, but only two were notably successful: his original libretto of *Le Vaisseau Fantôme* (*The Flying Dutchman*, 1842), based on Richard Wagner's *Der fliegende Holländer*, and *Le Pacte de Famine* (*Hunger's Pact*, 1839).

Foucher may have been guilty of some gaucheries but he managed to write one almost perfect play, *Notre-Dame de Paris*, first performed at L'Ambigu Comique in 1850. His first adaptation actually gave the novel a happy ending! But, some years later, he and Paul Meurice rewrote it to conform to the novel.

Victor Hugo and Paul Meurice

Paul Meurice:

A graduate of the Charlemagne College, Paul Meurice (1820-1905) was introduced to Victor Hugo by Charles Vacquerie in 1836 and quickly became his friend. He was also on friendly terms with Alexandre Dumas *père* and must have been a fairly good diplomat to remain on good terms with two men who were often at odds due to their professional jealousy.

A prolific playwright, Meurice produced at least one work of note every year: *Benvenuto Cellini* (1852), which later became the basis for the libretto of Saint-Saens' eponymous opera, *Schamyl* (1854), *La Famille Aubry* (1857), the classic swashbuckler *Fanfan la Tulipe* (1858), *Le Maître d'école* (1858), *François-les-bas-bleus* (1863), *Les Chevaliers de l'esprit* (1869), *Le Songe de l'amour* (1869), etc. With Dumas, Meurice collaborated on a French adaptation of *Hamlet* (1848) and *Les Deux Dianes* (*The Two Dianas*, 1845).

About the latter, Gothic author Jules Janin told this story to the Goncourts, and Paul Foucher retold a similar version in his memoirs:

One day, Meurice came to see Dumas in need of money. If he could only have 40,000 francs by the next day, he could make a brilliant marriage. Dumas was willing, but unable.

"I don't have ten percent of that sum available at the moment," he said.

"But your signature on a new novel can easily command an advance on royalties worth 50,000 francs," retorted Meurice.

"But," lamented Dumas, "I don't have anything ready at the moment."

Whereupon, Meurice smiled, having foreseen that possibility, and pulled out a manuscript box containing the novel *The Two Dianas*, which he later would dramatize.

Dumas thought for a moment and said:

"Leave it here, come back in the morning."

The next day, Meurice had his 40,000 francs and went on to be richly, and hopefully happily, married.

Meurice was a staunch Republican and wound up spending ten months in prison in 1848 for printing an article on the right of asylum in his newspaper, *L'Evenement*. The article was by Charles Victor Hugo, Victor Hugo's son. In 1869, he co-founded the journal *Rappel*, and handled literary and theatrical criticism. There, he worked with the young Emile Zola.

During Hugo's exile to the Channel Islands, Meurice was his "man in Paris," taking care of all his business. He wrote (or co-wrote) stage adaptations of Hugo's famous works: *Notre-Dame de Paris* (with Paul Foucher), *Les Misérables* (with Charles Victor Hugo) and *Quatre-Ving Treize*. All three plays are very faithful and powerful dramatic works.

Between 1880 and 1885, Meurice directed the publication of Hugo's collected works. After Hugo's death, as his literary executor, he edited and published *The Love Letters of Victor Hugo* (1896) and set up the Victor Hugo Museum on the Place de Vosges in Paris.

The Hunchback of Notre-Dame:

The play that Foucher and Meurice drew from the novel is quite extraordinary. It tracks the novel carefully, never betraying it, and yet is enormously effective as a play. This perhaps reflects the theatricality of Hugo's works in the novel form. Like Shakespeare, Hugo has a way of drawing characters that makes them unforgettable from their first appearance. And the two adaptors bring this out. It's not just Quasimodo who is unforgettable, so is Esmeralda, and so, in his twisted way, is Claude Frollo, and the Beggar-King in the Court of Miracles.

Thanks to Lon Chaney, Charles Laughton and Walt Disney, Quasimodo has become almost a household word for humpbacked, animal ugliness. But beneath the ugly exterior, he is, in a retarded sort of way, desperate for love and affection, and many generations of readers and moviegoers have loved this character. His very inability to articulate his feelings makes him sympathetic.

It is possible that Quasimodo owes something to Shakespeare's Caliban, but unlike Caliban, he is good. Shakespeare would have loved this work.

Characters

Quasimodo the Hunchback, bell-ringer of Notre-Dame
Esmeralda, a Gypsy dancing girl
Dom Claude Frollo, Archdeacon of Notre-Dame
Phoebus de Chateaupers, Captain of the King's Guards
Pierre Gringoire, a poet
Jehan Frollo, a student and Claude's younger brother
Robin Poussepain, another student and Jehan's friend
Clopin Trouillefou, a beggar and King of the Court of Miracles
Madame de Gondelaurier, a wealthy Parisienne
Fleurs-de-Lys de Gondelaurier, her oldest daughter, engaged to Captain Phoebus
Colombe de Gondelaurier, her second daughter
Diane de Gondelaurier, her third daughter
Berangere de Gondelaurier, her youngest daughter
Gervaise, the wife of a Parisian armorer
Oudarde, Gervaise's friend
Mahiette, Gervaise's friend, visiting from Reims
Eustache, Mahiette's son
Jacques Coppenole, a bourgeois of Ghent
François Chanteprune, a beggar
Bellevigne de l'Etoile, another beggar
La Sachette, the Recluse of the Tour Roland
Tristan L'Hermite, Provost of the King's Guards
Pierrat Torterue, Official Torturer and Executioner
La Falourdel, a landlady
Various Students, Guards, Monks, Vagabonds, Beggars and other Parisians.

Paris, 1482.

Act I

Scene I
The Grand Hall

To the left is a dais in gold brocade. To the right is a marble table supported by a carpenter's frame, the upper surface of which serves as a theater stage. A tall tapestry hides the interior vestry. A ladder is placed against the table. At the back, there is a small door surmounted by a round window. A large crowd of students and bourgeois already fill the hall. Students enter tumultuously from the back.

STUDENTS: Students! All of you, make room for the students.
JEHAN FROLLO (*above at the cornice of a pillar*): Ho! Friends. Ho! Robin Poussepain!
ROBIN POUSSEPAIN: Heavens! Is that Jehan Frollo? What the Devil are you doing perched there on that cornice?
JEHAN FOLLO: I like to be on top of things.

(*Enter from the left, Mahiette, Gervaise and Oudarde.*)

MAHIETTE: Oh! What a crowd! What an uproar! Gervaise, what's this enormous table made of marble?
GERVAISE: It's there for the Morality Play.
MAHIETTE: The Morality Play? What's the Morality Play?

GERVAISE: You don't know what a Morality Play is, my poor Mahiette? What have you been learning at your University in Reims?
OUDARDE: A Morality Play is a Mystery.
MAHIETTE: A Mystery?
GERVAISE: Yes, a play for speaking characters. The one they're going to give is for the marriage of Monseigneur the Dauphin. It's called *The Good Judgment of Madame the Virgin*.
MAHIETTE: And when is it going to start?
OUDARDE: Anytime now. They're waiting until noon and for the arrival of the Flemish Ambassador.
MAHIETTE: Oh, noon will arrive on time, but the Ambassador? I'm not so sure... Look, the dais is still empty.
OUDARDE: Look! Someone is starting to arrive.

(*Enter from the left, Madame de Gondelaurier and her daughter, Fleur-de-Lys, followed by Captain Phoebus*.)

MAHIETTE: Ah, the magnificent attire!
GERVAISE: It's Madame de Gondelaurier with her daughter, Fleur-de-Lys.
MAHIETTE: And that handsome Captain accompanying them? Do you know his name?
GERVAISE: I do indeed. He bought his arms at my husband's shop. He's Captain of the King's Guards, Monsieur Phoebus de Chateaupers.
PHOEBUS (*turning*): Did I hear my name? Heavens! Gervaise, the pretty armorer.
JEHAN FROLLO: Hello there, Captain! Hello, friend Phoebus.
PHOEBUS (*aside*): It's that sly devil, Jehan Frollo.
JEHAN FROLLO: Captain! Say, you look like you are on fatigue duty. (*laughter in the crowd*)

MADAME DE GONDELAURIER (*to Phoebus*): Nephew, why do you force us to pass through these jeering students and all these braying, ill-bred men?
MAHIETTE: They seem to like taking him down a notch, that friend of Gervaise!
OUDARDE: He's a gallant and joyous soldier, but completely broke! The money-lenders won't leave him anything but his name.
GERVAISE (*sighing*): And even that, he's going to be forced to give up, in exchange for a rich dowry from his cousin, Fleur-de-Lys.
MAHIETTE: You call that *giving up*, my poor Gervaise? You really *are* naive!

(*The clock strikes noon. There is uproar and movement in the hall.*)

OUDARDE: Ah! Noon at last.

(*A great, expectant silence ensues.*)

JEHAN FROLLO: Well, what about the Mystery? Isn't it going to start?
ALL: The Mystery! The Mystery!
GRINGOIRE (*beaming, putting his head through the fold of the curtain*): O intelligent people! O generous impatience! How they know to sniff out a masterpiece.
JEHAN FROLLO (*shouting*): The Mystery now! Or else, I think we should hang the Provost from the top of the rafters–in lieu of comedy and morality.
CROWD: Well said! And burn down the theater, too!
GRINGOIRE (*uneasy*): Ay! Their ardor is going a bit too far.

ROBIN POUSSEPAIN (*shouting*): Burn it down! And bring a rope for the Provost!
JEHAN FROLLO: And for the actors! (*rumblings of approval*)
GRINGOIRE: A rope for the actors! What about my play then? Let's put an end to this nonsense.

(*He comes out from behind the curtain and climbs up the ladder.*)

CROWD: Silence! Silence!
GRINGOIRE (*on the marble table, with energetic bows*): Mesdames and Messieurs of the bourgoisie...
JEHAN FROLLO: Who the Hell are you? Yes, you, the one doing all the talking.
GRINGOIRE: My name is Pierre Gringoire. I have the good fortune to be the author of the very beautiful Morality Play that is indeed going to be declaimed and performed before you very soon...
JEHAN FROLLO: Not very soon. Right away!
CROWD: Right away! Right away!
GRINGOIRE: His Eminence, the Cardinal of Bourbon–
CROWD: The Mystery! The Mystery!
GRINGOIRE: –And the Ambassador from Flanders.
CROWD: Burn! Burn!
GRINGOIRE: Burn? That's enough! We will start right away. (*coming down the ladder*)
CROWD: Hurrah! Hurrah!
GRINGOIRE (*aside*): Let's buy some time.

(*He goes back between the curtain.*)

PHOEBUS (*approaching the three women*): Hello, Gervaise.

GERVAISE (*joyfully*): Monsieur Phoebus! What, you dare leave your fiancée?
PHOEBUS: Oh. Her mother is too boring.
GERVAISE: Yes, but the daughter is too pretty.
PHOEBUS: Bah! I'll have plenty of time to look at her later. All my life! Whereas you, Gervaise– (*he whispers to her laughing*)
MAHIETTE (*to Oudarde*): He is a terribly bold fellow, that Captain.
GERVAISE (*low to Phoebus*): What honeyed words! Meanwhile, it's been like a century since I've last seen you.
PHOEBUS: It's because I owe your husband for a coat of mail and two short swords. Ah, if it was to you I could pay them... I would go to see you no later than last week!
GERVAISE: Yes, but you stopped *en route*. Place Baudoyer.
PHOEBUS: Ah. You saw me.
GERVAISE: Yes. Our back room gives on the square. And on that square, whenever you arrived, the Gypsy woman danced.
PHOEBUS: What Gypsy woman?
GERVAISE: You know very well! Esmeralda!
PHOEBUS: Ah yes. The little dancer with the goat.
GERVAISE: Yes! Yes! And noticing her, you stopped your horse and she interrupted her dance.
PHOEBUS: She's not unpleasant to look at, that little wild girl. But I swear to you, Gervaise, I've never said a word to her. I am amorous only of your sweet eyes. When do you want me to prove it to you?
GERVAISE: Oh. Your future mother-in-law is looking this way.

PHOEBUS: Yes. A storm's brewing. (*low and quick to Gervaise*) I will come tomorrow to make my peace.
CLOPIN TROUILLEFOU (*one-armed, extending his hand to Phoebus*): Charity if you please!
PHOEBUS: Go to the Devil (*leaving*)
JEHAN FROLLO: Hey! Hey! You're stalling, you rascals! The play!
CROWD: The play! The play!
JEHAN FROLLO: Start now or we'll set fire to the theater!
GRINGOIRE (*aside*): And the Ambassador who hasn't arrived yet! This is bad! (*aloud*) We're starting, gentlemen, we're starting! (*music from inside the scaffolding*)
GERVAISE (*in a low voice to Mahiette, pointing to Gringoire*): He's the author, you know. The author of the Mystery.
GRINGOIRE (*who has overheard*): The author, yes, ladies! And we're going to start! I'm going to wrap myself in all my glory.
OUDARDE: If you mean your frock, it needs to be seriously mended.
GRINGOIRE (*casting a disdainful look at his smock coat*): Bah! Why should such trivialities matter? Once my Morality Play has been performed, the Provost will count me out 12 sols.
CLOPIN TROUILLEFOU (*extending his hand to him*): Charity if you please.
GRINGOIRE: Sorry, my friend, I haven't had lunch yet. But come back tonight and I'll be rich. Tonight, I will dine. Ah, here come the actors of the Prologue.

(*The curtain rises. Enter four characters in half-yellow, half-white costumes. The first, dressed in linen, holds a spade in his hand; the second, in wool, a scales; the third, in brocade, a sword; the fourth, in silk, two golden keys. One after the other, they climb onto the stage.*)

CROWD: Hurrah! Hurrah!
MAHIETTE: What sort of Christians are these?
GRINGOIRE: Don't you know how to read? Their names are sown on the bottom of their costumes.
MAHIETTE (*reading*): Ah yes! Labor, Commerce, Nobility and Clergy. That's nice!
GRINGOIRE: And it's plain, too! Go, Labor. (*music inside stops.*)
LABOR: Good folks, I am Labor. I come to give–
CLOPIN TROUILLEFOU (*in a screeching voice*): Charity, if you please! (*laughter*)
JEHAN FROLLO: Hey! That's Clopin Trouillefou! Heavens! It must tire you to be bandy-legged, my friend, just as you are one-armed? (*more laughter*)
GRINGOIRE: The Philistines! Speak, Commerce!
COMMERCE: I am Commerce. Good city bourgeois that I am. We are returning–
USHER (*at the door to the left, announcing*): Monseigneur the Cardinal de Bourbon! (*all eyes turn toward the door*)
GRINGOIRE (*aside*): He couldn't get here sooner, the Cardinal!

(*The Cardinal climbs on the dais.*)

USHER: The Rector of the University.
JEHAN FROLLO (*thumbing his nose*): Hey! The Rector! Hey!
USHER: Monseigneur Louis de Graville, Admiral of France. The Ambassador of Flanders.

(*Everyone turns their back to the stage to observe the new arrivals.*)

GRINGOIRE: To have worked for faces and to see only backsides. To be a poet and to have only the success of an apothecary! Nobility! Try to speak! Very forcefully! Loudly! Very Loudly!
NOBILITY (*in a loud voice*): I am Nobility. We are looking, in the hills and the valleys, everywhere, for our dauphin...
USHER (*announcing*): Monsieur Jacques Coppenole, Clerk of the Alderman of the Illustrious City of Ghent!
COPPENOLE (*entering*): No, by the Cross! Jacques Coppenole, shoemaker. Nothing more, nothing less. Shoemaker. By the Cross, that's fine enough.
JEHAN FROLLO: Long Live Master Coppenole!

(*Coppenole thanks Jehan with a wave of his hand.*)

ALL: Vivat!
COPPENOLE (*noticing Clopin Trouillefou*): Ah, if I'm not mistaken, it's Clopin Trouillefou. Good meeting you, my friend! (*giving him his hand*)
ROBIN POUSSEPAIN (*with admiration*): Ah! He's not proud, that merchant.
ALL: Long Live Master Coppenole!

(*Coppenole takes his place on the dais.*)

GRINGOIRE: Your turn, Clergy. Carry the dullards off for me!
CLERGY: Our Dauphin, proud and handsome, true son of the Lion of France wanted–

COPPENOLE (*rising*): Hola! Excuse me, bourgeois and squires of Paris! What are those folk doing there on that stage? Are they going to speak words?
GRINGOIRE: Words! (*pained*) Oh, to call my verse mere words.
COPPENOLE: They'd do better to give us a Moorish dance or some other mummery. This is not what they told me. They promised me a Festival of Fools with the election of a Fools' Pope.
GRINGOIRE: The Mystery first! The Mystery!
JEHAN FROLLO: No! No! We want the Festival of Fools!
GRINGOIRE (*running back and forth in different tones of voice*): The Mystery! We demand the Mystery! The Mystery!
THE STUDENTS: The Festival of Fools!
COPPENOLE: Listen. We, too, have our Fools' Pope in Ghent. And in this, we are not behind, by the Cross! But, here, as we are–
GRINGOIRE: Don't listen to him! We want the Mystery!
JEHAN FROLLO: Let Master Coppenole speak!

(*Coppenole sends him a gesture of thanks.*)

ALL: Speak! Speak!
COPPENOLE: Amongst us, a crowd assembles like here, then each in his turn goes and puts his head through a hole and makes a face at the others. The one who is seemed to be the ugliest by the acclaim of all is then elected Pope. That's all. It's very diverting. Would you like to make your Pope after the manner of my country? That would be less tedious than listening to these chatterers. There's a sufficiently grotesque sample

of both sexes here so as to have us a real Flemish guffaw. And we have ugly enough faces so as to hope for a really pretty grimace.
ALL: Yes! Yes! Hurrah! Let's elect a Pope!
GRINGOIRE (*exasperated*): No! No! No!
JEHAN FROLLO (*pointing*): There's a round stone window over that door which seems to be made expressly for it.
ALL: Yes! Yes!
MADAME DE GONDELAURIER (*rising*): Come, child, Phoebus. I don't want to be present at such a gross spectacle.
PHOEBUS (*aside*): Just when it was becoming amusing!

(*He withdraws with his relatives*.)

MAHIETTE: Must we stay for this farce?
GERVAISE: That's something to see. And since you came all the way from Reims for that–

(*The first grimacing face appears in the window*.)

THE THREE WOMEN: Ah! How horrible! (*shouts and laughter*)
JEHAN FROLLO: He's not ugly enough! Let's have another!

(*A face appears in the window with enormous cheeks. The shouts and laughter redouble*.)

JEHANN FROLLO: Ah, that's cheating. He's got to show his full face.

(*The face opens its mouth and shows its teeth.*)

JEHANN FROLLO: That's quite a face! He's got a good chance.

(*Quasimodo's face appears in the window.*)

ALL: Hurrah! Hurrah!
COPPENOLE: Ah, that's a true Pope of Fools! (*thunderous applause*) Bring in the winner!

(*Quasimodo comes in from the rear. At his appearance, the applause redoubles.*)

COPPENOLE: Friends, he's superb. He's got what it takes to cause Proserpina, the Devil's wife herself, to have a miscarriage. But it must be very tiring for you to hold your face in that pose. Put it back in its usual condition. You will be ugly enough, still! He doesn't budge! Ah! Prodigy! The grimace is his true face! (*exclamations and acclamations*)

(*Jehann Frollo comes down from his cornice.*)

JEHAN FROLLO: Hey! Why, I recognize him! It's the bell ringer of Notre-Dame. It's Quasimodo.
OUDARDE: Oh! The horrifying hunchback!
GERVAISE: And as evil as he is ugly!
COPPENOLE: By the Cross, I've never in my entire life seen more magnificent ugliness! (*striking Quasimodo on the shoulder*) You are a character with whom I have had the desire to feast since I first heard of you–were it to cost me a dozen crowns. What do you say? Shall we dine together? Ah, indeed. I forget. You're deaf.

JEHAN FROLLO: Eh, yes. He has become deaf from the noise of the bells.
COPPENOLE: Oh! Devil of a man! It seems he's a hunchback as well. Yet he walks. He's a one-eyed, bandy-legged hunchback. He looks at you. You speak to him, but he's deaf. By the Cross, he'll make a wonderful Pope.
JEHAN FROLLO (*yelling in Quasimodo's ear*): Quasimodo! You've been proclaimed Pope of the Fools!
QUASIMODO (*laughing*): Ah, yes! Fine! Fine!
JEHAN FROLLO: Friends, the procession must be splendid and worthy of our monstrous new Pope. A true Triumph!
ALL: A Triumph! A Triumph!

(*Everybody presses around Quasimodo for whom they quickly improvise a makeshift throne at the back of the stage.*)

GRINGOIRE: Malediction! They're all going to leave. (*to the three women*) You aren't planning to be part of this abominable cortege?
MAHIETTE: No, certainly not.
GRINGOIRE: Then you are true friends of the muses. We'll start the Mystery all over again.
A STUDENT (*looking through the window into the square*): Esmeralda! Esmeralda!
GERVAISE: Esmeralda. The dancer with the goat! Come, come, Mahiette. We can't miss this!

(*The three women leave. Gringoire watches them go in despair.*)

GRINGOIRE (*with sadness*): O Apollo! They've taken away my glory. And my supper.

(*Meanwhile, Quasimodo is raised on a kind of platform and they carry him laughing and dancing around him with cries of "Hurrah!"*)

CURTAIN

Scene II
The Fools' Pope

The Place du Petit Pont, opposite side of the Seine River from Notre-Dame. To the left, there is a house supported by wood pillars. At the corner of the street, one notices a pretty statue of the Virgin Mary inside a niche behind an iron grille; below it, a commemorative candle is burning. At the back of the stage, the crowd mills around, hiding Esmeralda and her goat.

GERVAISE (*to Oudarde and Mahiette, who enter left from the back*): Come on! Hurry up! Esmeralda has started her performance, but I think she's only doing her card tricks so far. What kept you so long?
OUDARDE: It's Mahiette! At the corner of the Rue Mouton, she stopped in front of the Tour Roland. I was unable to tear her away from it.
MAHIETTE (*looking behind her*): What was that face I saw behind the bars of a lower window and which disappeared immediately?
OUDARDE: Why, I told you. It's Sachette, the Recluse from the Rat-Hole.
MAHIETTE: Is she a prisoner?
GERVAISE: No. She shut herself up there voluntarily. She took a vow of penitence.
MAHIETTE: Has she been there a long time?
OUDARDE: It's been 15 years.
MAHIETTE: Why is she called Sachette?
GERVAISE: Because all she wears for clothes is an old sack.
MAHIETTE: Even in the winter?

OUDARDE: Even in the winter.
MAHIETTE: Poor woman!
GERVAISE: It's said that she locked herself in there after some kind of great sorrow, but it's as if it gives her pleasure to retain her sorrow.
MAHIETTE: But what was this sorrow? Does anyone know?
OUDARDE: No. No one knows.
MAHIETTE: Well, perhaps I know... We will return to see her.
GERVAISE: Whenever you like.

(*Suddenly, the crowd applauds. We hear Esmeralda tune up her drum.*)

GERVAISE: Ah! The Basque drum. Esmeralda has finished her card tricks. She's going to sing.

(*The crowd opens to let Esmeralda through. The goat is at the back, squatting on a mat.*)

ESMERALDA (*singing in Spanish*): Un cofre de gran riqueza / Hallaron dentro un pilar / Dentro del nuevas banderos / Con figuro de espantar. * Alarabes de cavallos / Sin poderse menear / Con espades y los cuellos / Bellestas de buon echar.

(*More applause from the crowd.*)

MAHIETTE: Oh. What a sweet charming voice.
GERVAISE: She's going to dance and her dance is better than her singing.

(*Esmeralda begins to dance to the accompaniment of the Basque drum. After a moment, Claude Frollo enters and, hidden in the crowd, casts a deep contemplative glance over the dancer.*)

CLAUDE FROLLO (*in a dark voice*): Look. Look at her. Hell's very own daughter.
MAHIETTE: Who was that talking?
OUDARDE: I don't know. Someone who wanted to annoy the girl.
GERVAISE: He really succeeded. See, she's stopped. But she's starting again.

(*The crowd applauds. Gringoire arrives.*)

GRINGOIRE: They are applauding? Alas, not my Mystery. (*looking*) No, it's a dancing girl. (*admiringly*) What was I saying? Not a girl, a goddess.
CLAUDE FROLLO: A witch!
MAHIETTE: That voice again!

(*The dance ends in the midst of applause.*)

ESMERALDA (*to her goat, presenting him her Basque drum*): You turn, Djali.
GERVAISE: Watch carefully now, Mahiette. Here is the goat's number.
ESMERALDA (*to the goat*): Djali, what month are we in?

(*Djali paws the drum four times with his hoof.*)

OUDARDE: It's true. We are in April.
GRINGOIRE: See what they prefer to poetry!

ESMERALDA: Djali, what day of the month are we?

(*The goat raps five times.*)

ESMERALDA: What time of day is it?

(*The goat raps six time; at the same time, the bells ring six. Applause.*)

MAHIETTE: It's marvelous.
CLAUDE FROLLO: There's some witchcraft behind it.
ESMERALDA (*to herself, shivering*): Oh! I fear that voice is as sinister as the man behind it.
CROWD: The goat again. One more time!
ESMERALDA: How does Master Charmolue, the King's Prosecutor, plead in Court?

(*The goat starts bleating and waving his front hoof. More laughter and applause.*)

CLAUDE FROLLO: Sacrilege! Blasphemy!
ESMERALDA (*with terror*): Ah! It's that evil man again.

(*The applause continues. She collects the audience's money in her drum.*)

GRINGOIRE: Oh! The fire spirit! The nymph! The Bacchante of Mount Menaleen! (*Esmeralda presents her drum to him. He puts his hand in his jacket and shakes his head*) Alas, I lack the gold.

(*Jehan Frollo, Quasimodo and their entourage enter.*)

JEHAN FROLLO: Make way! Make way! Come, fools! Follow me, wenches! Shout Hurrah! Sing Hallelujah! If not, may the Devil take you and may our Pope bless you!

(*The cortege moves in: musicians playing strange instruments, vagabonds, students, etc. In the center, the "Pope"'s guards, with candles on their shoulders, bear the platform upon which Quasimodo sits, with cross, cape and mitre!*)

CLAUDE FROLLO (*recognizing Quasimodo*): Quasimodo!

(*He rushes into the crowd and tears the mitre and the cross from the Hunchback's hand.*)

CLAUDE FROLLO: How dare you! Take these off at once!
GRINGOIRE: Dom Claude Frollo! The Archdeacon of Notre-Dame!
JEHAN FROLLO: My brother!

(*Quasimodo, furious, jumps off the platform.*)

MAHIETTE: Ah, my God! The monster's going to tear him apart.

(*Quasimodo lunges towards Claude Frollo, but at the last minute, recognizes him, then stops.*)

QUASIMODO: My master.

(*He falls to his knees. Claude Frollo tears his cape and mitre from him.*)

CROWD: Down with the Priest! Death to him! He's insulting our Pope! The Pope of Fools!

(*Hoots, threats and fists raised against Claude Frollo.*)

QUASIMODO (*with a deep roar*): Don't dare touch my master!
CLAUDE FROLLO (*calm, to Quasimodo*): Wait for me here. I'll be right back.

(*He leaves to the left. Quasimodo protects his retreat, throwing his fists in the air.*)

JEHAN FROLLO: Show some respect for the Archdeacon, my brothers! And pity him too, for I suspect he's been fasting.
GRINGOIRE: Just like me, then! (*noticing Esmeralda moving away*) I'm going to follow her. If she's a goddess, she'll lead me to Heaven; if she's a mortal, she'll lead me–somewhere to eat.

(*He follows Esmeralda.*)

JEHAN FROLLO: My friends, we've lost our venerable Pope. I offer you another in replacement, less ugly but infinitely meaner, which should make up for it. And that successor is–me!
ALL: Hurrah! Long Live Pope Jehan Frollo!

(*They lift him on the platform and a procession begins to form. Night is falling. The candle before the Virgin Mary is lit. The stage empties, except for Quasimodo.*)

QUASIMODO (*alone*): What bad luck my master showed up. He got angry. He tore my beautiful gold clothes. Why? There were so fine. I was happy and proud. Never in my life have I enjoyed such pleasure. Always around me, I see, I feel only scorn, hate, outrage and disgust. Today, they applauded me, they admired me, they bore me in triumph like a King. But it must've been bad since the master was angry. It's a shame!

(*Claude Frollo returns.*)

CLAUDE FROLLO: You're still here? Good! (*to himself*) The girl must eventually return and cross over that bridge to get back home to her kind at the Court of Miracles. This place is dark and empty. Come now, I must deal with this wretched passion that's devouring me. I've struggled mightily, but fate is stronger yet. Let me have this woman and the Devil can take me. Hell with her will be like Heaven to me. (*he taps Quasimodo on the shoulder.*) Follow me into the light. (*they walk to the shrine to the Virgin Mary*) Deaf to almost any sounds, you know how to read my lips, so look at me and listen.
QUASIMODO: I'm looking and I'm listening.
CLAUDE FROLLO: You remember to whom you owe your wretched life?
QUASIMODO: A man who lives alone with only his thoughts never forgets. It was 20 years ago today that I was left inside the wood basket for abandoned children hanging from the door of Notre-Dame. A poor, little

malformed creature who frightened and horrified all who saw him. They said, “It’s a monster. It’s a demon. Best throw him in the river. Best throw him in a fire.” But a young priest came, extended his hand and said: “I shall adopt this child.” And indeed, he sheltered him, fed him and raised him. It was between the legs of that young priest that the boy sought refuge when dogs and children howled after him. It’s from that young priest he learned to speak, to read and to write. And when he became a man, the priest entrusted him with the bells of Notre-Dame, those angelic voices which come to him again and again when his ears are covered, these friends which cradle him with their heavenly music. The young priest was you, master. The monster was me. You see, I have not forgotten.

CLAUDE FROLLO: Do you also remember how to express gratitude?

QUASIMODO: The whole world hates me, and I hate the whole world. But you, I love. Whatever you desire, I wish it. Whatever you wish, I will do. To my deformed members, God gave prodigious strength to allow me to serve you better. I am your servant, your slave, your dog, your creature. Do you call this gratitude? I feel it’s merely my duty.

CLAUDE FROLLO: So you will do what I am going to order you to do, without question?

QUASIMODO: I don’t know if I will succeed, but I’ll die trying–or have it done.

CLAUDE FROLLO: Very well. Someone’s going to pass this way soon. Man or woman, he must be carried off as I order.

QUASIMODO: A man at the end of my fists may struggle in vain over my head. A woman, I can carry under my arms, folded like a scarf.

CLAUDE FROLLO: Fine! I don't need to explain why I give you this order.
QUASIMODO: No, master. You are wisdom, you are science, you are virtue. You cannot wish something unjust; you cannot order that which is not good.
CLAUDE FROLLO: Excellent. (*cupping his ear*) That little bell is that of the goat which accompanies her. Let's hide behind these pillars and wait for my signal.

(*They conceal themselves. Esmeralda enters with her goat. Gringoire follows her, at a distance.*)

ESMERALDA: Come, Djali, come on. You were begging to go home.
GRINGOIRE (tired): She keeps going on and on. But she's got to live somewhere. Gypsies have a good heart. Who knows?
ESMERALDA (*to Djali*): Is it that thin shadow behind us that's frightening you?
GRINGOIRE: Ah! She's finally stopping.
ESMERALDA (*to Gringoire*): Who are you? You really ought to stop frightening Djali by following us.
GRINGOIRE: I only frighten the goat?
ESMERALDA: Look, what do you want? You've been following us since the Croix-Rouge.
GRINGOIRE: Yes.
ESMERALDA: Are you still going to follow me for a while?
GRINGOIRE (*hand on his stomach*): I feel that I cannot do otherwise. I'm so hungry!
ESMERALDA (*pointing to the right*): You would follow me even over there?
GRINGOIRE: What's over there?

ESMERALDA: The Court of Miracles, the City of Gypsies, the realm of cutthtroats and burglars where I live; a sewer of vice, a kingdom of sin whose subject I am.
GRINGOIRE: I would willingly become its subject, too.
ESMERALDA: But you're not–do you speak *Argot*?
GRINGOIRE: I confess I don't.
ESMERALDA: And not being an *Argotier* yourself, you still want to enter their kingdom?
GRINGOIRE: With you at my side, yes!
ESMERALDA: Oh, you can enter. Nothing could be simpler.
GRINGOIRE: Ah? Thanks.
ESMERALDA: Only, I warn you, you won't be able to leave.
GRINGOIRE: The Devil!
CLAUDE FROLLO (*to Quasimodo*): Go!

(*Quasimodo rushes Esmeralda.*)

GRINGOIRE: Help! Help!

(*Quasimodo gives him a slap of his backhand that sends the writer reeling four feet away on the pavement.*)

GRINGOIRE: Ouch! I see stars... Candles... Thirty-six candles!

(*He remains stretched out on the pavement, unconscious. Meanwhile, Quasimodo seizes Esmeralda who struggles bravely.*)

ESMERALDA: Murder! Murder!
CLAUDE FROLLO: Come!

(*Suddenly, Pheoebus enters on horseback, followed by archers bearing torches.*)

PHOEBUS: Halt right there, wretches, and release that woman!

(*Quasimodo releases Esmeralda and tries to flee, but is surrounded by the archers who seize him and bind him. Esmeralda seeks refuge by the horse of Phoebus. Claude Frollo flees into the night.*)

PHOEBUS: My beautiful child. You see what happens when one runs around all alone in the streets at night.
ESMERALDA (*recognizing him*): Captain Phoebus!
PHOEBUS (*dismounting*): Esmeralda.
ESMERALDA (*joyfully*): You know my name?
PHOEBUS: Indeed. After all, you know mine!
ESMERALDA: Oh, I'm but a poor Gypsy girl. For me to know the name of a brave and handsome young Captain is nothing. But you?
PHOEBUS: Well, if today's the first time I've spoken to you, I confess it's not the first time I've seen you. I admire you greatly. That is to say, I–
ESMERALDA (*stopping him*): Don't say it so soon! I can't believe it! And it would be too sad, for I'm so happy.
PHOEBUS: You are happy?
ESMERALDA: Yes! For this is our first meeting and you just saved me! I owe you–who knows?–perhaps more than life.
PHOEBUS: So what will you give me instead?
ESMERALDA: Oh Captain!
PHOEBUS: Perhaps I'm entitled to a small advance, eh? A kiss... (*trying to kiss her*)

ESMERALDA (*recoiling*): Oh, no! Mercy!
PHOEBUS (*persisting*): A single kiss. That's nothing.
ESMERALDA (*still recoiling*): Nothing for you, alas, but everything for me.
PHOEBUS: Heavens! Look into my eyes and see if I don't love you. Look!
ESMERALDA: I don't even want to look into myself.
PHOEBUS: Stop, wicked girl! Love is meant to enter your heart.
ESMERALDA: Love tonight, but misfortune tomorrow.

(*She slips out of his arms and flees. Phoebus pursues her for a few feet, then returns.*)

PHOEBUS: She's escaped! Truly, a fine adventure! (*looking at Quasimodo*) The dove has flown away, only the crow remains. That one will pay double.

(*He gets back on his horse and rides away, with the archers leading off Quasimodo.*)

GRINGOIRE (*regaining his senses*): Where am I? Where's the dancing girl? Gone! I'm sore and numb. Hey! What are those shadows coming over there?

(*Three beggars, one blind, one one-eyed, one crippled emerge from several hiding places.*)

FIRST BEGGAR (*low*): The guards have gone.
SECOND BEGGAR: Yes, but the curfew bell hasn't rung yet.
GRINGOIRE: Where's that breeze coming from? Ah, I'm freezing. No wonder–I was lying in the gutter! I noticed on the Rue de la Savatière, a stepping stone to put

on one's slippers. For want of better, it will serve me as a pillow.

(*The three beggars notice him and approach him.*)

FIRST BEGGAR: La buona mancia, signor! La buona manria.
GRINGOIRE (*looking at him*): May the Devil take you, and me with you if I know what you're saying.

(*He starts to leave but only bumps into the Second Beggar.*)

SECOND BEGGAR: Señor Caballero, para comprar un pedaso de pan.
GRINGOIRE: It's a barbaric tongue that he speaks, too. And he's luckier than I because he understands it. (*looking at him*) That's not a man, that's a gallows pole.

(*As he escapes, he bumps into the Third Beggar.*)

THIRD BEGGAR: Facitote caritatem?
GRINGOIRE: Now, there's one who speaks a Christian language! My friend, I sold my last shirt. Or, since you speak the language of Cicero, Vendidi meam ultimam chemisam! And in case you don't understand, look! (*turns out his pockets to show they're empty*) Is that clear enough? Now, goodnight!

(*He wants to pass. Suddenly, the curfew sounds.*)

THE THREE BEGGARS: The curfew!

(*They all rush Gringoire.*)

GRINGOIRE: What’s this? The cripple’s running after me! The blind man bars my passage. The one-armed man puts two hands on my collar! What do you want from me? Where are you taking me?
THE THREE BEGGARS (*pulling him*): To the Court of Miracles.

CURTAIN

Scene III
The Court of Miracles

A vast, irregular-shaped square, enclosed by old houses with worm-eaten facades. Some fires around which make for a grim atmosphere. Broken tables stand here and there. To the left, there is a big tankard; to the right, a wooden gibbet.

CLOPIN TROUILLEFOU (*entering furious*): Hell and damnation! Is that all you've stolen?
BELLEVIGNE: Yes, Sire, King of Thieves.
CLOPIN TROUILLEFOU: It would be better to beg! And the sick, my trained pretender–what did you get in the way of alms? Come forward, Chanteprune.
CHANTEPRUNE: Here's the total, Sire, reviewed and certified by the Duke of Egypt and the Emperor of Gallilee. Seventen *sous*.
CLOPIN TROUILLEFOU: What misery!
BELLEVIGNE: The curfew just sounded. All the late comers have now returned.
VOICE (*outside*): To the King! Let's take him to the King!

(*The blind beggar, the cripple and the one-eye man bring in Gringoire*.)

BLIND MAN: Majesty, here's a scamp who tried to enter the Kingdom of Argot without being an Argotier. He was in the neighborhood after curfew.
CLOPIN TROUILLEFOU: Scoundrel. What do you have to say in your defense?

GRINGOIRE: Majesty, Sire... How am I to address you?
CLOPIN TROUILLEFOU: Sire, His Majesty, or comrade, call me what you wish, but be quick about it.

(*He scrambles onto the cask and sits on a stool.*)

GRINGOIRE: I am the one who, this morning–
CLOPIN TROUILLEFOU: By the Devil's claws! Your name, wise guy, and nothing else. You're before three powerful sovereigns. Myself, Clopin Trouillefou, King of Thieves, successor of the grand Coesre in the Kingdom of Argot, Mathias Hunyadi Spicali, Duke of Egypt, and of Bohemia, that old man that you see there with a rag around his head, and Guillaume Rousseau, Emperor of Galilee, that fat guy there who's not listening to us and is caressing a trollop. We three are your judges. You have violated the privileges of our Court. You must be punished unless you are a prig, a cadger or a stroller, that is to say in the argot of honest men, a thief, a beggar or a vagabond. Justify yourself. Are you something like that?
GRINGOIRE: Alas, I have not the honor... I am an author.
CLOPIN TROUILLEFOU: That suffices. You're going to be hanged. It's very simple. The punishments you honest bourgeois use against us, we use on you. So it's your fault if it is bad. It's necessary, from time to time, to see the grimace of an honest man in a hangman's noose. That makes the whole thing honorable. (*laughter among the crowd*) Come on, friend, share your rags merrily with these young fellows before you swing.
GRINGOIRE: Sire, Emperors and Kings, you can't be thinking of such a thing! I am the poet who put on the Morality Play this morning at the Grand Hall!

CLOPIN TROUILLEFOU: Ah! I was there, and if it was your work, master poet–
GRINGOIRE (*aside*): I am saved!
CLOPIN TROUILLEFOU: –Since you bored us this morning, we have double the reason to hang you tonight.
GRINGOIRE: But–
CLOPIN TROUILLEFOU: Look, let yourself be hanged and no more dilly-dallying.
GRINGOIRE: Pardon me. It's worth the trouble.
CLOPIN TROUILLEFOU: No, it isn't! I don't see why you care about being hanged. It happens all the time. Yes, I can see how it would seem appalling to you, but that's only because you bourgeois aren't accustomed to it. So you make a big thing of it.
GRINGOIRE: Not at all! Not at all!
CLOPIN TROUILLEFOU: After all, it's not like we wish you any harm. Still, I'll tell you what: there may be a way to get yourself out of the predicament–for the moment. Would you like to become one of us?
GRINGOIRE: Would I like to? Most assuredly!
CLOPIN TROUILLEFOU: You agree to become a member of the Court of Miracles?
GRINGOIRE: A member of the Court. Precisely.
CLOPIN TROUILLEFOU: A member of the free men?
GRINGOIRE: Of the free men!
CLOPIN TROUILLEFOU: A subject of the realm of Argot?
GRINGOIRE: Of the realm of Argot!
CLOPIN TROUILLEFOU: A vagabond?
GRINGOIRE: A vagabond!
CLOPIN TROUILLEFOU: Mind you, you won't be hanged any the less for all that! (*laughter*)
GRINGOIRE: The Devil!

CLOPIN TROUILLEFOU: Only, you will be hanged somewhat later, with more ceremony, at the expense of the good city of Paris and by honest men. It's a consolation.
GRINGOIRE: So be it! I want to be a vagabond, a thief and a bum! Whatever you wish.
CLOPIN TROUILLEFOU: It's not a matter of will. Good will doesn't put an extra onion in the soup. To be received in the Kingdom of Argot, you must prove you are good at something, and for that you must search the dummy.
GRINGOIRE: I will search the dummy as much as you like.

(*At a sign from Clopin, two men bring a dummy hung with little bells and big bells, which they hang from the scaffold.*)

CLOPIN TROUILLEFOU (*pointing to a stool*): Climb up there.
GRINGOIRE (*after having tried*): The Devil! I'm going to break my neck. Your stool limps like bad verse. There's no way for a poet to cling to it.
CLOPIN TROUILLEFOU: Will you get up there!

(*Gringoire manages to get up on the stool.*)

CLOPIN TROUILLEFOU: Now place your right foot over your left leg and stand on tiptoe.
GRINGOIRE (*trying and staggering at each attempt, in the midst of laugher*): Do you absolutely insist that I break a leg, Sire?
CLOPIN TROUILLEFOU: Listen, friend you talk too much. Here's what you have to do in short. You're going

to stand on tiptoe as I told you, in such a way as to be able to reach the pocket of that dummy. You will search it, you'll pull out a purse that's there, and if you do all this without causing any bells to ring, that's fine, you will be one of us.
GRINGOIRE: But if I make the bells ring?
CLOPIN TROUILLEFOU: You will take the place of the dummy. Come on, hurry up!
GRINGOIRE (*extending his hand, then stopping*): And if a little wind comes up?
CLOPIN TROUILLEFOU: You will be hanged too.
GRINGOIRE: Oh, to think my life depends on the least of these bells. Oh bells, please don't ring. Clappers, please don't clap. Don't ring, don't tinkle, little bells...

(*He stands on tiptoe, touches the dummy, extending his arm; then, he loses his balance and automatically grabs the dummy. The bells ring all together. Hoots and laughter. Gringoire falls on his face.*)

GRINGOIRE: I am dead!
CLOPIN TROUILLEFOU: Pick the clown up and hang him for me right away.

(*They grab Gringoire, put the rope around his neck and force him to stand on the stool.*)

CLOPIN TROUILLEFOU: Now, on the count of three, when I clap my hands, Red Audry, you will push the stool to the ground. Chanteprune, you will hang on the legs of the rogue. Bellevigne, you will throw yourself on his shoulders. All three at once. Are you ready?
GRINGOIRE: Mercy!
CLOPIN TROUILLEFOU: Are you ready?

ALL THREE: Yes, Sire!

(*He claps twice, then stops.*)

CLOPIN TROUILLEFOU: Ah, one moment, I was forgetting–there's a custom that we don't hang a man without first asking if there's a woman who wants him. Comrade, it's your last chance. You must marry one of our girls or it's the rope.
GRINGOIRE: Everything considered, I would prefer the girl.
CLOPIN TROUILLEFOU: Hola, ladies! Is there a strumpet among you who will have this good-for-nothing poet? Colette-la-Charonne! Elisabeth Trouvain! Simone Jodouyne! Marie Piédebou! Thonne la Longue! Bérarde Fanouel! Michelle Genaille! Claude Ronge-oreille! Mathurine Girorou! Hola! Come and have a look! A man for nothing! Who wants one?

(*Three women emerge from the throng and come to look at Gringoire. The first is a big wench, with a square face.*)

A FAT GIRL (*examining Gringoire's clothes*): Let's see your cloak.
GRINGOIRE: I lost it.
FAT GIRL: Your hat.
GRINGOIRE: They took it from me.
FAT GIRL: Your shoes.
GRINGOIRE: They hardly have any soles left.
FAT GIRL: Then let yourself be hanged and say thanks.

(*The next, a hideous old crone, walks around Gringoire.*)

GRINGOIRE (*looking alternatively at the crone and the gibbet*): The horrible witch! I believe I'm hesitating.
OLD CRONE: Nah. He's too skinny.

(*The third, a younger girl with a sympathetic air, approaches.*)

GRINGOIRE: Please, save me!
YOUNG GIRL (*after a moment's hesitation*): I can't! Guillaume Longuejoue would beat me.
CLOPIN TROUILLEFOU: Friend, you're mighty unlucky. No one wants him. Going once! Twice! Three Times! Gone!
SHOUTS AMONG THE VAGABONDS: Esmeralda! Esmeralda!

(*Esmeralda comes in with her goat.*)

GRINGOIRE: Esmeralda!
ESMERALDA (*considering Gringoire in silence for a moment*): You're going to hang this man?
CLOPIN TROUILLEFOU: Yes, sister. Unless you take him for your husband.
ESMERALDA: I take him.

(*The crowd is stupefied.*)

GRINGOIRE (*as he is released*): This is a dream.
CLOPIN TROUILLEFOU: Bring me a jug. (*a jug is brought*)
ESMERALDA (*presenting it to Gringoire*): Smash it to the ground. (*the jug breaks in four pieces*)

CLOPIN TROUILLEFOU: Brother, she's your wife. Sister, he's your husband. For four years. Go. We leave you now to your wedding night. Vagabonds, let them be escorted, and don't forget tomorrow at the break of day we must go congratulate the newlyweds–except the bride.

CURTAIN

Scene IV
A Wedding Night

Esmeralda's room. Gothic vaults. There is a door on the left and a door in the back, a table, a trunk and a long chest of drawers. Also a few stools.

(*Gringoire enters followed by Esmeralda, lamp in hand, and her goat.*)

GRINGOIRE: This is your room?
ESMERALDA: It's my room.
GRINGOIRE: I ask your permission to sit down.
ESMERALDA (*indifferently*): As you like.

(*She leads the goat to the room on the left, puts down her drum, lights a candle and arranges the stools.*)

GRINGOIRE (*seated, following her with his eyes, aside*): So that's Esmeralda! A celestial creature! A street dancer! So much and so little. It was she who dealt the deathblow to my Mystery this morning and she who saved me tonight. My evil genius, my good angel! On my word, what a ravishing girl! And who must love me madly to have taken me that way.
ESMERALDA (*sitting, day-dreaming*): Phoebus!
GRINGOIRE (*aside*): By the way, I don't know much about how this sort of thing is done, but I am her husband. (*rising and going to her; aloud*) Adorable Esmeralda...
ESMERALDA: What do you want from me, then?
GRINGOIRE: Can you ask me that?

ESMERALDA: I don't know what you mean! (*rising*)
GRINGOIRE (*aside*): She doesn't know? Bah! After all, I have no business with a virtuous maid. From the Court of Miracles! (*aloud*) Am I not your sweet friend; aren't you mine?

(*He goes to her and takes her by the waist. She slips out of his hands and turns, a small dagger in her hand.*)

GRINGOIRE: Aie!
ESMERALDA: You must be a very bold clown!
GRINGOIRE (*speechless*): Oh, excuse me, Mademoiselle! But why did you take me for your husband?
ESMERALDA: Should have I allowed you to be hanged?
GRINGOIRE: So you had no other thought in marrying me than to save me from the gibbet?
ESMERALDA: And what other thought could I possibly have had?
GRINGOIRE (*aside*): I see! I'm not yet so triumphant in love as I thought. But then, what was the good of breaking that poor jug? (*aloud*) Let's compromise, then. I swear by my share of Heaven to not approach you without your leave and permission. But give me something to eat.
ESMERALDA (*bursting out in laughter*): Oh, as to that, willingly.

(*She goes to the trunk and brings forth bread and cheese, apples and an earthenware jug of beer which she places on the table.*)

GRINGOIRE (*aside*): I'm going to eat! Indeed, my stomach is suffering more than my heart. (*sitting at the table and eating avidly*) Aren't you eating?

(*She makes a negative hand gesture, her eyes fixed on the ceiling. She remains in that pose, day-dreaming.*)

GRINGOIRE (*aside*): What the Devil is she so preoccupied with? It can't be that grinning stone gargoyle carved in the ceiling. Damn! I could bear that comparison! (*coughs*) Hum! hum! (*aloud*) So you didn't want me for your husband?
ESMERALDA: No.
GRINGOIRE: For your lover?
ESMERALDA: No.
GRINGOIRE: For your friend?
ESMERALDA: Perhaps.
GRINGOIRE: Do you know what friendship is?
ESMERALDA: Yes. That's being brother and sister. Two souls who touch each other without mingling. Two fingers on one hand.
GRINGOIRE: And love?
ESMERALDA: Oh! Love. That's being two and yet only being one. A man and woman who blend into an angel. That's Heaven.
GRINGOIRE: What must one be then, to please you?
ESMERALDA: One must be a man.
GRINGOIRE: What about me then? What am I?
ESMERALDA: A man has a helmet on his head, a sword in his hand and golden spurs on his heels.
GRINGOIRE: I see! A man is not a man without a horse. Are you in love with someone perhaps?
ESMERALDA: Love?
GRINGOIRE: Love.

ESMERALDA: I will know that soon.
GRINGOIRE: And why not tonight? Why not with me?
ESMERALDA: I can only love a man who can protect me.
GRINGOIRE: I see. Pardon my foolish absence of mind. By the way, how did you escape from the clutches of Quasimodo?
ESMERALDA (*hiding her face in her hands*): Oh, the horrible monster.
GRINGOIRE: Horrible indeed. But how were you able to escape him? (*Esmeralda smiles without responding*) Do you know why he was following you?
ESMERALDA: No, I don't. But you, too, were following me. Why were you?
GRINGOIRE (*embarrassed*): Hum! I no longer recall. Why do they call you Esmeralda?

(*She pulls from her bosom a little oblong bag, suspended from her neck by a string of beads. It is covered with green silk and bears in its center a large piece of green glass, in imitation of an emerald.*)

ESMERALDA: I'm not sure why. Perhaps because of this little bag.

(*Gringoire extends his hand toward it.*)

ESMERALDA: Don't touch it. It's an amulet. You can harm the charm, or the charm may injure you.
GRINGOIRE: Who gave it to you? (*Esmeralda puts a finger over her lips*) That suffices. You're not French?
ESMERALDA: I don't know.
GRINGOIRE: Do you know at least how old you were when you came to France?

ESMERALDA: Quite small.
GRINGOIRE: And to Paris?
ESMERALDA: Last year.
GRINGOIRE: Do you have parents?
ESMERALDA (*humming, head back, eyes to Heaven singing*): My father is a gull. My mother is a gannet. I crossed the water without a skiff. I crossed the water without a boat. My mother is a gannet. My father is a gull.
GRINGOIRE: I see. Anyway, your name matters little now that you have the right to bear mine.
ESMERALDA: Yours! I don't even know what it is!
GRINGOIRE: If you want it, here it is: Pierre Gringoire, at your service.
ESMERALDA: I know a prettier one.
GRINGOIRE: Wicked girl! But perhaps you'll love me when you get to know me better. Learn first of all of my birth. I am the son of a scrivener of Gonesse. Only, my father was hanged by the Burgundians and my mother was disembowelled by the Picards. Orphan, with no soles for my feet except the paving stones of Paris, what was I to do? What condition to take? Soldier? I wasn't brave enough. Monk? I wasn't devout enough. And also, I don't like to drink. I had no inclination to be a teacher. True, I can't read, but that's not a reason. In short, seeing that I was good for nothing, I set myself up as a poet and composer of rhymes. It's a job one can always take when one is a vagabond, and it's better than stealing as some young brigands, friends of mine, advised me. You're listening to me, right? One day, at last, I had the good fortune to meet the Reverend Archdeacon of Notre-Dame, Dom Claude Frollo.

ESMERALDA (*awakening from her reverie, terrified*): Claude Frollo! Oh! I know him! I know him!
GRINGOIRE: He took an interest in me. And it's to him that I owe my being a truly learned man today. I was the author of a Mystery that was played lately with great triumph at the Great Hall. It'll make me lots of money–if they pay me for it. I also wrote a 600-page book on the comet of 1465–the one that made a man insane. You see, I am not a bad catch for marriage. So I am at your service, Mademoiselle–myself, my wit, my science and my letters. Ready to live with you as you please. Chastely or happily, husband and wife if you find it good; brother and sister if you find it better.
ESMERALDA (*falling back into her revery*): Phoebus. Phoebus. What does that mean?
GRINGOIRE: It's a Latin word which means "sun."
ESMERALDA (*rising*): Sun!
GRINGOIRE: It was the name of a handsome archer who was also the Sun God.
ESMERALDA (*repeating passionately*): The Sun God.

(*She leaves slowly; at first, Gringoire does not notice he is alone*.)

GRINGOIRE: And under another name, Phoebus is Apollo, the God of Poets, the God of Harmony, the God that I–Heavens! She's no longer here! (*hearing the noise of a bolt*) She's locked herself in. (*with a grimace*) Chastity! But at least, has she left me a bed? This chest, perhaps? Bah! I'm falling asleep (*stretching out on the chest*) Ah! How hard it is! Come on! Resign yourself to it. But that sure was a strange wedding night. (*he closes his eyes*).

(*Suddenly, he leaps up. A terrible charivari can be heard outside. Clopin enters with five or six vagabonds.*)

CLOPIN TROUILLEFOU: Brother, it's day. They're giving you a serenade outside to celebrate your conjugal bliss.
GRINGOIRE: Ah–what a good idea!
CLOPIN TROUILLEFOU: I have to inform you of one thing. If, in a year, you haven't brought your tribute to our Court in the form of a strong and clever son, or a daughter of dazzling beauty, or even a two-headed child, you will be hanged.
GRINGOIRE: Again!

(*The Charivari starts up again.*)

CURTAIN

Act II

Scene V
The Danger of Confiding One's Secrets to a Goat

The house of Madame Gondelaurier, hung in Flemish tapestry, fawn-colored leather with gold foliage. The beams of the ceiling are painted in gold. To the left is a tall fireplace with hanging coats of arms and shields. To the opposite right is a window, with a balcony giving on the Square of Notre-Dame. In the back, there is a large door with a tapestry curtain. All around are armoires with porcelain, faience, stained glass, etc.

Madame de Gondelaurier is sitting in a great oak armchair. Phoebus stands near her, with a bored and irritated look, polishing the pummel of his sword with his deerskin leather glove. Three of Madame's daughters, Fleur-de-Lys and the younger Colombe and Diane, are seated on low stools and working on their needlepoint. The fourth, Berangere, stands on the balcony, looking on the Square.

MADAME DE GONDELAURIER (*looking at Fleur-de-Lys adoringly*): Captain Phoebus, have you ever seen a face more lovely and more cheerful than your betrothed's? Isn't she more light-skinned and more blond than any other girl in Paris? Doesn't she have accomplished hands? And that neck, isn't it ravishing to the point of being shaped just like a swan's?
PHOEBUS (*distracted*): That, it is.

MADAME DE GONDELAURIER: Isn't my darling Fleur-de-Lys beautiful to the point of adoration?
PHOEBUS: That, she is.
MADAME DE GONDELAURIER: Why, stop polishing your sword and go say something to her. You've become quite timid lately.
PHOEBUS: Timidity is neither my virtue nor my fault.
MADAME DE GONDELAURIER: Then get going.

(*Phoebus goes to Fleur-de-Lys.*)

PHOEBUS (*aside*): What am I going to say to her? I've got to find something gallant to say. (*aloud*) Beautiful cousin, what's the subject of your needlepoint?
FLEUR-DE-LYS: Handsome cousin, I already told you three times. It's Neptune's grotto.
PHOEBUS: Ah. And who is this gendarme who's blowing a trumpet with all his cheeks?
FLEUR-DE-LYS (*annoyed*): That's Triton.
PHOEBUS: Why does your mother always wear an armorial coat like our grandmothers in the time of Charles VII? Her brocaded laurel makes her look like a walking mantelpiece.
FLEUR-DE-LYS: Is that all you have to tell to me?
MADAME DE GONDELAURIER (*watching them, aside*): A touching picture of love!
BERANGERE (*on the balcony*): Ah, look, mother! There's the pretty dancing girl who danced on the Square of Notre-Dame the other day. She's playing her drums for the bourgeois and the peasants.
FLEUR-DE-LYS: Pah! Some Gypsy from Bohemia!
COLOMBE AND DIANE (*rising*): Let's see! Let's see.
PHOEBUS (*aside, motionless in the middle of the room*): I can hear her Basque drum... But I don't dare go

near the window. Ah! A pox on all these obnoxious manners.
FLEUR-DE-LYS (*aside*): Perhaps I've made him angry? (*aloud*) Handsome cousin! Didn't you tell us of a Bohemian girl whom you rescued last night from a dozen creatures?
PHOEBUS: Oh, there was only one creature, cousin. A horrifying hunchback, the bell-ringer of the Cathedral, from what they told me. Imagine the insolence! He was carrying off the girl like a ragdoll, this monster. But he'll pay dear for it. The scoundrel will spend today on the Place de Greve at the tender mercies of the Paris Executioner.
FLEUR-DE-LYS: She was lucky that you were there to save her. Why, perhaps it's she who's dancing there. Come see if you recognize her.

(*She takes his arm and leads him to the window.*)

PHOEBUS (*excitedly*): Yes, it's her! I recognize her!
FLEUR-DE-LYS: So you took a careful look at her last night?
PHOEBUS: Er, I recognize her by her goat.
DIANE: Oh, the pretty little goat, really!
BERANGERE: Are its horns made of real gold?
FLEUR-DE-LYS: Phoebus, since you know this Bohemian girl, signal her to come up. That will amuse Berangere.
ALL THREE YOUNG GIRLS (*clapping their hands*): Oh, yes! Yes! Please!
PHOEBUS: Why, that's ridiculous. She's undoubtedly forgotten me already.
FLEUR-DE-LYS: No one forgets you that way, handsome cousin.

PHOEBUS: Well, if you insist, I'll give it a try. (*leaning over the balcony and calling*) Girl! Girl!
BERANGERE: Oh, she has heard you! She's coming! She's coming here.
FLEUR-DE-LYS (*aside*): She was quick enough to obey a sign from Phoebus.
DIANE: Who's that man all in black standing in the gallery of the Tower of Notre-Dame?
PHOEBUS: That's the Archdeacon, Dom Claude Frollo.
DIANE: See how he follows the girl with his eyes.
PHOEBUS: Like a hawk looking at a sparrow.
FLEUR-DE-LYS: Let the Gypsy take care of herself for the Archdeacon doesn't love Gypsies.
BERANGERE: Ah! Here she is! Here she is!

(*Esmeralda enters, then stops, intimidated, at the threshold.*)

DIANE: Ah! She's very pretty.
FLEUR-DE-LYS: Yes, in a rather common sort of way.
ESMERALDA (*glancing at Phoebus, aside*): He's not looking at me.
MADAME DE GONDELAURIER (*in her armchair*): They tell me you're the girl my nephew rescued the other night. Do you recognize Captain Phoebus?
ESMERALDA: Oh, yes!
MADAME DE GONDELAURIER: Come closer, little one.

(*Esmeralda, staring at Phoebus, doesn't hear.*)

BERANGERE: Come, Mademoiselle.

(*Esmeralda finally comes closer.*)

PHOEBUS: You ran away rather quickly last night, my pretty! Did I frighten you?
ESMERALDA: Oh no!
PHOEBUS (*turning on his heels in a low voice*): She's ravishing.
FLEUR-DE-LYS: But dressed like a savage.
DIANE: Her skirt's short enough to make you quiver.
PHOEBUS (*aside*): All the bitches are snapping at the doe.
ESMERALDA (*aside*): They make fun of me–before him! Why did I come up here? (*to Mme de Gondelaurier*) Will that be all, Madame?
MADAME DE GONDELAURIER: No. What possesses you, girl, to run in the streets dressed this way, without a proper shirt or slip?
PHOEBUS (*aside, impatiently*): Aren't they going to leave her alone! (*aloud*) Bah! Let them talk, girl. Your dress is a bit wild and outlandish, but why should a delightful girl like you care?
ESMERALDA (*aside*): He's defending me.
MADAME DE GONDELAURIER (*rising*): Phoebus!

(*Suddenly, the goat ambles in, following its mistress.*)

MADAME DE GONDELAURIER: Holy Virgin! What have we here? Ah, the ugly creature! Spare me that hideous beast.
ESMERALDA: It's only Djali, Madame.

(*She takes it and puts it on her knees to caress it.*)

BERANGERE: This little goat has horns of gold.

DIANE (*low, to Fleur-de-Lys*): They say this Bohemian is a witch and her goat performs miracles.
FLEUR-DE-LYS: Gypsy, make your goat perform a miracle!
ESMERALDA (*uneasily*): I don't know what you mean.
DIANE: A miracle, magic, sorcery.
FLEUR-DE-LYS (*pointing to a little pouch worn by the goat*): What's that it's got on its neck?
ESMERALDA (*rising*): That's my secret.
FLEUR-DE-LYS (*aside*): I'd really like to know what it is.
BERANGERE (*aside*): If I could only see what's inside that pouch!
MADAME DE GONDELAURIER (*irritated*): Look here, girl, if you and your goat aren't going to dance for us, what are you doing here?
ESMERALDA (*insulted*): Nothing, indeed. Madame is right.

(*She starts to leave.*)

PHOEBUS (*stopping her*): By the Cross! You can't go like this. Dance something for us, my pretty.
FLEUR-DE-LYS: Why don't you call her by her name, Phoebus. Surely you must know her name?
MADAME DE GONDELAURIER: Yes, what's your name, girl?
ESMERALDA: Esmeralda.

(*The women laugh.*)

DIANE: Now there's a dreadful name for a girl.

MADAME DE GONDELAURIER: Your parents obviously didn't fish that name out of the baptismal font, my dear.

(*Meanwhile, young Berangere has led the goat into a corner of the room, opened the pouch and pulled out an alphabet of letters which she has spread on the floor. Suddenly, she lets out a scream.*)

BERANGERE: Ah! Mother! Fleur-de-Lys! See what the goat just wrote.
DIANE: A word written by a goat!
MADAME DE GONDELAURIER: A word!
FLEUR-DE-LYS (*reading*): "Phoebus."

(*Esmeralda retrieves Djali.*)

ESMERALDA: Ah! Djali, you've betrayed me!
PHOEBUS (*aside, delighted*): My name!
FLEUR-DE-LYS (*weeping*): So that's her secret! Ah, mother, she's a witch!
MADAME DE GONDELAURIER: What's the matter with you? That's no reason to weep.
FLEUR-DE-LYS (*low to her mother*): She's my rival! She's bewitched him!

(*She staggers and faints.*)

MADAME DE GONDELAURIER: My daughter! She's fainted. (*to Esmeralda*) Get out!
PHOEBUS (*low to Esmeralda*): At nightfall. At the foot of Pont Saint-Michel.
ESMERALDA (*low*): What are you saying?
PHOEBUS (*low*): I'll be there.

MADAME DE GONDELAURIER (*chasing Esmeralda out, furiously*): Get out of my house! Get out! Bohemian from Hell!

CURTAIN

Scene VI
The Pillory

The Place de Greve. To the left is a house on pillars, seen from the side. In the back, we see the Seine and the Island of La Cité with Notre-Dame in the distance. To the right, is the Tour Roland; on the first floor, there is a barred window with the inscription *Tu Ora*. Center stage is the pillory.

Enter Gervaise and Oudarde with Mahiette holding a big boy, Eustache, by the hand. In his other hand, Eustache has a large cake.

GERVAISE: This is the Place de Greve, Mahiette.
MAHIETTE: Where is Sachette's cell?
OUDARDE (*pointing to the barred window*): There it is.
MAHIETTE (*to the boy*): Eustache, I see you nibbling on the cake. You know we're bringing it to the Recluse. She lives in the Rat-Hole of the Tour Roland. And that's the pillory, right?
GERVAISE: Yes. Have you ever seen someone pilloried, Mahiette.
MAHIETTE: Yes, in Reims. Many times.
GERVAISE: Ah! Bah! But I bet that your pillory in Reims is but a harmless cage where they only whip a few peasants.
MAHIETTE: Not so! We've had some very famous criminals. Folks who killed both their mothers and fathers. The man they'll be whipping today is nothing to write home about.

GERVAISE: Well, yes, today is only an ordinary whipping. The punishment of that bell-ringing monster who tried to carry off a woman.
MAHIETTE: Not even a woman, a Gypsy!
OUDARDE: You don't like Gypsies, do you, Mahiette?
MAHIETTE: They frighten me. Especially when I have my boy with me.
OUDARDE: Why?
MAHIETTE: Because they steal children.
OUDARDE: What is odd is that Sachette shares the same notion about Gypsies. No one knows where this comes from. She especially detests Esmeralda who isn't even bad. Whenever the dancer passes through the Place, she shouts all kinds of curses and insults at her.
MAHIETTE (*seizing Eustache's head with both her hands*): My Eustache–I don't want to happen to me what happened to Paquette Chantefleurie.
GERVAISE: Who's that?
MAHIETTE: It's a story from Reims.
GERVAISE: Tell me anyway.
MAHIETTE: Indeed, you should hear it before we talk to the Recluse. Well, 15 years ago, Paquette Chantefleurie was a pretty girl living with us. Her life was far from ordinary, but we took pity on her because she had been orphaned quite young and was very poor. One day, she had a child, a little baby girl whom she adored, and who was so pretty that people came from afar just to see her. Eustache! I told you not to nibble on the cake! For sure, that baby girl was given more linens and embroidery than any Kings on Earth. Among other things, she received a pair of slippers that even King Louis XI would have been jealous of. They were the two prettiest little red slippers I've ever seen. Just about the length of my thumb–you had to see the child's feet come out of them

to believe they could have gotten inside them. She was a darling! Her mother became more and more crazy about her every day. She hugged her, covered her with kisses, ate her up. She lost her head over her. She thanked God everyday for that baby.

GERVAISE: So far the story's good and beautiful but where are the Gypsies in all this?

MAHIETTE: Wait. One day some very peculiar folks came to Reims–beggars, vagabonds who came straight from Egypt by way of Poland, telling fortunes in the name of the King of Algiers. They would look in your hand and make prophecies to astonish a Cardinal. The poor Chantefleurie was filled with curiosity. She wanted to know her daughter's fate and took her to the Gypsies. And the Gypsy women admired the child and kissed her and marveled over her little hand. They made a show of her pretty feet and pretty slippers. They told the mother her child would become a beauty, a lady, a queen. Paquette Chantefleurie returned proudly to her garret. The next day, while her child was napping, she ran to tell a neighbor that her baby would one day dine at the same table as the King of England, the Archduke of Ethiopia and a hundred other wonders. She left the door slightly ajar. On her return, she found it wide open. She ran to the bedroom. It was empty. The child was there no more.

OUDARDE: Ah! My God!

GERVAISE: Nothing else?

MAHIETTE: Yes. They found one of the little red slippers. The mother rushed outside, screaming: "My child! Who has my child? Who took my child?" She went through the town, ferreted out all the streets, ran around madly the whole day, in a terrible state, peering at doors and windows, behaving like a wild beast who has lost its

curs. She stopped passers-by, screaming: "My daughter. Who has my daughter?" She met the Abbot of St. Remy and said to him: "Father, I will plough the Earth with my very finger for the Church, but please, ask God to return my child to me." It was all heart-breaking. Suddenly, she started screaming: "The Gypsies! The Gypsies did it! Call the soldiers! Burn the witches!" But the Gypsies had already gone. It was a very dark night. They couldn't pursue them. The next day, Chantefleurie's hair had gone grey. And the day after that, she disappeared.
GERVAISE: And the little slipper?
MAHIETTE: The little slipper disappeared with her.
GERVAISE: Poor Chantefleurie. It's a terrible story. And I'm no longer surprised, Mahiette, that you have such fear of Gypsies.
EUSTACHE: Mother, can I eat the cake now?
MAHIETTE: No! We're going now to give it to the Recluse.
EUSTACHE: But it's *my* cake!
GERVAISE: We shouldn't look into the hole all at the same time for fear of startling Sachette. She knows me a little. I am going to see how she is.

(*She goes softly and looks through the window.*)

MAHIETTE: Well?
GERVAISE: She's crouching motionless on the flagstones, her arms crossed, her knees pulled against her chest. You would think she's made of stone. She's looking fixedly at something in the corner.
MAHIETTE: Can you see what she's looking at?
GERVAISE: No, I can't.
OUDARDE: Speak to her. Try to get her to come to the window.

GERVAISE (*calling*): Sachette! You must be cold; would you like a little fire?
OUDARDE: She doesn't reply.
GERVAISE: She's making a negative sign. Well, at least take this corn pancake. And have a drink. It'll refresh you.
SACHETTE (*without being seen*): Yes. Some water.
MAHIETTE: Was it she who spoke?
GERVAISE: Yes. She's getting up. *(to Sachette*) Here, take this cake.
SACHETTE: Corn bread!
GERVAISE (*giving her an item of clothing*): Here's a chale against the cold. Put it over your shoulders.
SACHETTE: A chale!
EUSTACHE: She ate my cake! (*Oudarde grabs him and shakes him*) Er, bonjour, madame.
SACHETTE (*appearing at the window*): Ah, don't show me other people's children.
GERVAISE: You lost a child then?
SACHETTE: Yes. My daughter. The Gypsies stole her from me.
OUDARDE: Ah! That's why you hate them so much?
SACHETTE: Oh, yes, I hate them. One especially. The young one who's about the same age as my daughter would be, if her mother hadn't killed her. Each time that young viper passes in front of my cell, she makes my blood boil.
MAHIETTE (*to Gervaise and Oudarde*): Do you know this woman's real name?
GERVAISE: No. Just Sachette.
OUDARDE: Or the Recluse.
MAHIETTE: Well, me, I'd give her another name.
OUDARDE: Which one?

MAHIETTE: Watch! (*leaning towards the window and calling*) Paquette! Paquette Chantefleurie!
SACHETTE (*rushing to the window wildly*): Who's calling me? Is that you, Gypsy? Oh, take away that child. The Gypsy is going to pass! (*she disappears again*).
GERVAISE: A fortunate guess! How did you recognize her, Mahiette?
MAHIETTE: Do you know what she was looking at, so intently, in the corner? What I really thought I saw when I first arrived?
GERVAISE: What was it?
MAHIETTE: The little slippers!
GERVAISE: Ah! Poor woman!
MAHIETTE (*hugging Eustache*): Poor mother!

(*A crowd comes in, singing.*)

CROWD SINGING: A rope for the gallows bird, a birch for the monkey.
GERVAISE: Ah! They're bringing in the condemned.

(*Jehan Frollo enters, his arms linked with Robin Poussepain's and two other students*.)

JEHAN FROLLO: Make way! Make way! For our old Pope has fallen from triumph to torture.

(*The Guards push back the crowd and lead Quasimodo, who walks in wearing a sleeveless chemise, his arms tied behind his back. Tristan L'Hermite, the Provost of the King's Guards, and Pierrat Torterue, the official Torturer and Executioner of Paris, follow him, the latter a whip with long thongs in his hand. There are hoots and laughter from the crowd.*)

QUASIMODO: What do they want from me?

(*The Guards make him mount the pillory platform.*)

JEHAN FROLLO: What a boorish dolt. He understands his fate no more than a beetle locked in a box.
MAHIETTE (*to Gervaise*): Who's that man in the red uniform?
GERVAISE: That's Messire Tristan l'Hermitte, the Provost of the King's Guards. And with him is Master Pierrat Torterue, the official Torturer and Executioner of Paris.
MAHIETTE: What is the Provost putting there, by the stake?
GERVAISE: An hourglass. After having been whipped, the condemned must remain exposed in the pillory for an hour.

(*The Guards force Quasimodo to his knees. They remove his shirt and doublet, baring his upper body, and secure him to a circular plank; meanwhile, the Hunchback offers no resistance.*)

JEHAN FROLLO: Bourgeois and peasants, come and see. They are going to peremptorily whip Quasimodo, the bell-ringer of my brother, the Archdeacon. A comedian built like oriental architectural, with a domed back and two twisted columns for legs.

(*Laughter from the crowd. The Torturer stamps his foot. The wheel-like device to which Quasimodo is attached begins to turn. When it reaches Torterue, he applies the whip to Quasimodo's back.*)

QUASIMODO (*with a scream of pain and rage*): I don't want it! (*at the second turn and the second blow, he makes a violent but useless effort*) Why? Why?
JEHAN FROLLO (*clapping his hands around his mouth and shouting*): Because you tried to carry off a woman, stupid brute.

(*At the third blow, Quasimodo lowers his head, closes his eyes and thereafter remains totally impassive.*)

MAHIETTE: Let's get out of here! I can't watch this; it makes me sick.
GERVAISE: Wait! The Provost is holding out his baton. The scourging's over.

(*At a sign from the Provost, the Torturer, who was about to strike again, lowers his arm. The wheel stops. A soldier throws a yellow cloth over Quasimodo's shoulders.*)

JEHAN FROLLO: Only three blows. He was just starting to enjoy it.
ROBIN POUSSEPAIN: Here, take that, you evil monster! (*he throws a stone at Quasimodo*)
CROWD SINGING: A rope for the gallows bird, a birch for the monkey.

(*Gringoire enters from the left.*)

GRINGOIRE: Ah! It's that frightful Hunchback who almost killed me the other night. They're whipping him. I'm comfortable with that. (*noticing the cake in*

Eustache's hands) O what a delightful cake. Why don't you eat your cake, my little friend?
EUSTACHE: Mother doesn't want me to.
GRINGOIRE (*breaking off a big piece of the cake*): You must always obey your mother.
EUSTACHE: Mother! Someone else's eating my cake! Mother! She's not paying any attention. Good! Then, I'll eat the rest!
QUASIMODO (*in a pitiful tone*): Water!
ROBIN POUSSEPAIN: Would you like me to wet a sponge for you in the gutter?
JEHAN FROLLO (*to Robin*): Shut up! Dom Claude Frollo's here! My brother!
WOMEN: The Archdeacon.
QUASIMODO (*seeing Claude Frollo, uttering a scream of joy*): Ah! Master! My good Master! Ah! He's come to free me!

(*Claude Frollo enters.*)

QUASIMODO: Bless you, Master! I love you. You well know, you most of all, that I'm not guilty. Come, free me! Save me!

(*Claude Frollo who, at first, took some steps without seeing Quasimodo, recognizes him, then frowns and moves on.*)

QUASIMODO: Don't you hear me? Master! Please, don't leave! Help me!
JEHAN FROLLO: You heard your bell-ringer, my good brother?
CLAUDE FROLLO: What have I in common with this wretch?

(*He leaves.*)

QUASIMODO: Mercy!
AN OLD WOMAN: It's well done! You are a repugnant demon from Hell!
GERVAISE (*To Mahiette, who's overcome with pity*): What do you expect? He's been bad to all, all are bad to him.
QUASIMODO: Water!
ROBIN POUSSEPAIN: Here's a drinking cup! (*he flings a broken jug at the Hunchback's breast.*)

(*Enter Esmeralda, holding her goat.*)

CROWD: Esmeralda! Esmeralda!
QUASIMODO (*with a heart-rending scream*): Water!

(*Esmeralda stops and looks at Quasimodo.*)

QUASIMODO: The Gypsy girl! It's because of you that I'm here, you evil girl. I hate you. What have you come here to do? To avenge yourself, to add your blows to the crowd's? Water!

(*Esmeralda starts to go up the steps to the pillory.*)

QUASIMODO: Don't come near! Don't come near! I'll bite you.

(Esmeralda approaches Quasimodo who is snarling and grinding his teeth. She takes a gourd from her belt and presents it to the Hunchback's lips.)

ESMERALDA: Drink.

(*Quasimodo, stupefied, recoils.*)

ESMERALDA: Come on, drink!

(*Quasimodo drinks in huge gulps.*)

THE CROWD (*clapping their hands*): Hurrah! Hurrah!
SACHETTE (*rushing to the window*): The Gypsy! Cursed be you, child stealer! Cursed! Cursed!

CURTAIN

Act III

Scene VII
The Archdeacon's Cell

There is a garret window to the right and a door to the left. On a table are various instruments used for alchemy. Quasimodo is on his elbows, looking through the garret window onto the Square.

JEHAN FROLLO (*half-opening the door, discreetly*): It's I, brother... No one! His cell is empty. No, I was wrong, there is someone–Quasimodo! But no danger of that deaf man having heard me. What's he looking at so intently? Why, it's Esmeralda, dancing in the square. Oh! I hear footsteps. It must be the Archdeacon! Will he be inclined to let me have some money? I won't know right away.

(*He hides behind a curtain as Claude Frollo enters.*)

CLAUDE FROLLO: Why has she come back to dance on that very square? Is she trying to defy me? And that Gringoire who been with her since yesterday... What does it mean? I will find out. (*calling*) Quasimodo! Quasimodo! Hm, he seems completely lost in contemplation. His beastly eye bears a singular expression. Could he be looking at her, too? (*touching Quasimodo's hand*) Quasimodo!
QUASIMODO: Master!

CLAUDE FROLLO: You see that man down there, dressed in a yellow and red cassock, holding a goat near that dancing girl? Go down and tell him that Dom Claude Frollo would like him to come at once and speak to him.
QUASIMODO: I obey.

(*He heads towards the door.*)

CLAUDE FROLLO (*stopping him*): Quasimodo.
QUASIMODO: Master?
CLAUDE FROLLO: Yesterday, you called on me, Place de Gereve, but it wasn't in my power to save you. I couldn't spare you a moment of torture. I would have compromised my dignity. That's why I pretended to ignore you.
QUASIMODO (*somberly*): I understand. You did well.

(*He leaves.*)

CLAUDE FROLLO (*to himself*): I shall no longer look at her! Let's return to my books. (*sits at his table then pushes his books away*) Ah, for some time now, my mind has been unable to concentrate. I'm frustrated in all my experiments. A fixed idea possesses me and has withered my brain like a fiery trefoil. All it takes is one single wretched thought to render a man weak and mad. (*rising and taking some steps to the window*) Here, at this window, a poor heedless fly has just thrown itself into a spider's web. (*extending his hand*) Should I save it? No, let's leave it to its fate. Oh, this must be an omen. It flies and is happy, it searches for Spring, open air, liberty. But then, it crashes into the deadly web, facing the spider hanging from its hideous lair. Poor dancing girl.

Poor predestined fly. Alas, Claude, you're the spider, but you're also the fly. You were flying towards science, towards the Sun, towards eternal truth, but like the blind fly, senseless doctor, you didn't see this subtle spider's web hung by destiny between you and your goal. You're caught now, you wretched madman. And now you struggle, your head broken and your wings torn off, between the iron prongs of Fate. Let's leave, let the spider work its will!

(*He takes a compass from the table and gravely scratches letters on the wall. Jehan comes out of his hiding place.*)

JEHAN FROLLO (*to himself*): What's he scratching on the wall? It looks like a Greek word: ANANKE.
CLAUDE FROLLO (*turning upon hearing a noise*): Come in, Master Pierre.
JEHAN FROLLO: My dear brother–
CLAUDE FROLLO (*abruptly*): Ah, it's you, Jehan! What did you come here for?
JEHAN FROLLO: I came to ask you–
CLAUDE FROLLO: What?
JEHAN FROLLO: For a little moral support of which I am in need. (*aside*) And a little financial support which I need even more.
CLAUDE FROLLO: I'm very dissatisfied with you, Jehan.
JEHAN FROLLO: Alas!
CLAUDE FROLLO: Where are you in the Decretales of Gratien?
JEHAN FROLLO: I lost my notebook.
CLAUDE FROLLO: Where are you in the Latin Humanists?

JEHAN FROLLO: Someone stole my copy of Horace.
CLAUDE FROLLO: Where are you in Aristotle? Do you even know how to spell Greek properly?
JEHAN FROLLO: My reverend brother, would it please you if I were to translate in good French that Greek word written on the wall?
CLAUDE FROLLO: What word?
JEHAN FROLLO: ANANKE!
CLAUDE FROLLO (*strained*): Well Jehan, what does that word mean?
JEHAN FROLLO: Fatality! ANANKE, written in the same hand as that other word, AKATHARSIA, which means Impurity. You see that I know my Greek after all! (*a silence*) My reverend brother.
CLAUDE FROLLO: Look here! What is it you want?
JEHAN FROLLO: Well, it's this. I need money.
CLAUDE FROLLO: What for?
JEHAN FROLLO: Oh. I'm not coming to you with any bad intentions. It's not a question of playing the beau in the taverns with your cash. No, my brother, it's for a good work.
CLAUDE FROLLO: What good work?
JEHAN FROLLO (*trying to find a good work*): It's, er, for two of my friends, who would like to purchase an outfit for the child of a poorhouse widow. It will cost three *sous* and I want to contribute my share.
CLAUDE FROLLO: What are the names of your two friends?
JEHAN FROLLO: Pierre l'Assommeur and Baptiste Croque-Oison.[5]

---

[5] Peter the Slaughterer; and Baptist Crack-Gosling.

CLAUDE FROLLO: Singular names for charitable souls! And since when do poorhouse widows have brats to swaddle?
JEHAN FROLLO (*with effrontery*): Well, I also need money to buy a bracelet for the fetching Isabeau-la-Thierry.
CLAUDE FROLLO: Impure wretch.
JEHAN FROLLO (*pointing to the inscription on the wall*): AKATHARSIA indeed
CLAUDE FROLLO: Get out! I'm expecting someone.
JEHAN FROLLO: Brother Claude, at least, give me a little something to eat.
CLAUDE FROLLO: He who does not work shall not eat.
JEHAN FROLLO: OROROROROROI–
CLAUDE FROLLO: What does that mean?
JEHAN FROLLO: Why, it's Greek again. It's an anapest from Aeschylus, which perfectly expresses sorrow. Ah, I see that you're smiling! Good brother Claude, look at the holes in my socks.
CLAUDE FROLLO: I'll send you new socks but no money.
JEHAN FROLLO: Not even a poor little *sou*?
CLAUDE FROLLO: He who does not work–
JEHAN FROLLO (*with dignity*): Very well, my brother. But in that case, I'm distressed to have to tell you that I've received several fine offers and propositions from the Other Side. You won't give me any money? No? (*standing, his fist proudly on his hip*) Then, to the Devil it is and I'll become a criminal.
CLAUDE FROLLO (*after a moment of rage*): Become a criminal?
JEHAN FROLLO (*persisting*): Yes! This very day! (*going slowly to the door*)

CLAUDE FROLLO: Jehan! Do you know where you're going?
JEHAN FROLLO: Yes. To the tavern.
CLAUDE FROLLO: The tavern leads to the pillory.
JEHAN FROLLO: A lantern like any other.
CLAUDE FROLLO: The pillory leads to the gibbet.
JEHAN FROLLO: A scale which places a man on one side and the Earth on the other. It's fine to be a man.
CLAUDE FROLLO: The gibbet leads to Hell!
JEHAN FROLLO: Only another big fire.
CLAUDE FROLLO: Jehan! Jehan! The end will be bad.
JEHAN FROLLO: But the beginning will have been very good.

(*A knock at the door.*)

CLAUDE FROLLO: Someone's knocking. It's someone I'm expecting. I wish to be alone.
JEHAN FROLLO: Marvelous! I'm staying.
CLAUDE FROLLO (*aside, with a furious gesture*): Gringoire won't speak in front of him. (*aloud*) Hide yourself under this table and don't breathe a word!
JEHAN FROLLO: A *sou* to hold my breath.
CLAUDE FROLLO: Yes, later.
JEHAN FROLLO: I will listen first.

(*He hides under the table. Gringoire enters.*)

CLAUDE FROLLO: Come in, come in, Master Pierre. There you are, in a fine outfit. Half-yellow and red. like a ripe apple.
GRINGOIRE: It's indeed a wonderful attire, Archdeacon, and you see me more abashed than a cat wearing a calabash. What can I tell you, Reverend Master, the fault

lies entirely with my old jerkin, which cowardly abandoned me under the transparent pretext that it was falling to rags, and that it needed to go rest in a rag picker's basket.
CLAUDE FROLLO: Ha! So, what did I see! You, a philosopher, doing the job of a mountebank?
GRINGOIRE: I concede, Archdeacon, that it is a sad employment for one with my intellectual faculties, and that a learned man such as I shouldn't be made to spend his life playing the tambourine and carrying chairs in his teeth. But, alas, it's not enough to live one's life according to one's qualitios, one must also earn a living.
JEHAN FROLLO (*under the table*): Ah! A cramp! (*changing his position*)
CLAUDE FROLLO: How is it that you now find yourself in the company of that Gypsy girl?
GRINGOIRE: It's because she is my wife, Reverend Master, and I am her husband.
CLAUDE FROLLO (*grasping Gringoire's arms with fury*): Wretch! Could you have become so lost as to take the hand of that girl?
GRINGOIRE (*trembling*): Upon my place in Heaven, Reverend Master, I swear to you that I've never touched her, if that is what makes you so uneasy.
CLAUDE FROLLO: Why then do you speak of being husband and wife?
GRINGOIRE: Ah! Indeed. Because in the Court of Miracles, she married me over a broken jug to save my life. But this marriage has had no consummation, and my wife tricks me out of my wedding night every night.
JEHAN FROLLO (*under the table*): Heavens! Some bread.
CLAUDE FROLLO: How do you explain that?

GRINGOIRE: With some difficulties. It's all based upon some superstitious nonsense. My wife is a foundling, or a lost child, which is the same thing. She wears an amulet around her neck which–or so she believes!–will one day cause her to recognize her true parents, but which will lose its powers if the young girl loses her virtue. So it follows that we are both living very virtuously together.
JEHAN FROLLO: How hard this bread is!
GRINGOIRE: What's that crunching sound I hear down there?
CLAUDE FROLLO: A housecat regaling itself with some mouse. Pay no attention to it.
GRINGOIRE: Yes. All great philosophers have their little familiars.
JEHAN FROLLO: Thanks! And this one is even part of the family!
CLAUDE FROLLO: So you think, Master Gringoire, that this creature never has loved or loves any man?
GRINGOIRE: Hum! I think! I think! To doubt is the first precept of philosophy–and the prudence of husbands.
CLAUDE FROLLO: Why do you say this? Are you suspicious of somone?
GRINGOIRE: Well, there is a word that my wife often repeats to herself. A word that her goat is trained to write with moving letters. And this word might indeed be a name...
CLAUDE FROLLO: A name! What name?
GRINGOIRE: Phoebus.
JEHAN FROLLO: Heaven! Could it be my good friend the Captain?
CLAUDE FROLLO: And under this name, you suspect a man?

GRINGOIRE: Well, yes. Yesterday, toward dusk, we went to the Pont Saint-Michel, and there, a handsome Captain of the King's Guards graciously accosted us. They then obligingly sent me off with the goat.
CLAUDE FROLLO: A rendezvous.
GRINGOIRE: The first, indeed. But, by getting closer, I was able to hear that there is a second rendezvous planned–for tonight.
CLAUDE FROLLO: And you will let her go?
GRINGOIRE: If it's her wish, how do you expect me to prevent her?
CLAUDE FROLLO: What! Aren't you her husband? Haven't you every right over her?
GRINGOIRE: A few minutes ago, you didn't recognize any of my rights! In fact, you forbade me to be her husband!
CLAUDE FROLLO: To save her from evil, you wretch! To snatch her from the claws of Satan. You have more than a right, you have a duty. Go, run! Don't leave her for a moment. You will answer to me for her, on your life, on your very soul.
JEHAN FROLLO: Heavens! My brother's gone mad.
GRINGOIRE: But, Reverend Master–
CLAUDE FROLLO (*pushing him by the shoulders towards the door*): Don't question me! Go on! Go now, wretch! Perhaps it's already too late!

(*Gringoire leaves.*)

CLAUDE FROLLO: She loves another! Never! Ah! That idea overwhelms my whole being! That Gringoire is a pathetic fool, a coward. He won't know how to stop her. He won't dare face up that Captain. Ah, I'll go there myself. (*unhooking a long cloak from the wall.*) At least, let's hide under this Monk's cloak.

(*Jehan slides out from under the table, goes to the door, locks it and pockets the key. When Claude gets to the door after changing clothes, he finds Jehan standing in front of him.*)

CLAUDE FROLLO: Jehan! I'd forgotten you. (*reaching for the key*) Where's the key?
JEHAN FROLLO (*sarcastically, showing it*): Here it is.

(*Claude reaches for it. Jehan puts his other hand out.*)

JEHAN FROLLO: It'll be two *sous*.
CLAUDE FROLLO: You dare!
JEHAN FROLLO: Ask for three *sous*? Indeed I do!
CLAUDE FROLLO: Wretch!
JEHAN FROLLO: Come on! Five *sous*, my good brother.
CLAUDE FROLLO: Will you give me that key?
JEHAN FROLLO: Not under ten *sous*.
CLAUDE FROLLO (*tossing him a purse*): There you are! And go to Hell!

(*He leaves violently.*)

JEHAN FROLLO: I'm already there, my sweet brother, at the first stop on the way, at the tavern. To the tavern!

(*He, too, leaves joyfully.*)

CURTAIN

Scene VIII
The Demon Monk

A rather dismal-looking room. There are doors to the right and left. In the back, there is a large, half-opened window through which we see a view of the Seine and Paris in the moonlight.

The woman Falourdel enters, a candle in her hand, leading Phoebus and Jehan Frollo in.

LA FALOURDEL: Here's the room. But Monsieur knows it must be paid for in advance.
PHOEBUS: Yes, yes, my friend will pay you when he goes down. Leave us.

(*Exit La Falourdel left*.)

JEHAN FROLLO (*drunk*): Where are we, then? I have lodgings in the Rue Jean Pain Mollet–in vico Johannis Pain Mollet. You are hornier than a unicorn if you say otherwise.
PHOEBUS: Jehan, my friend, listen to me. I'm a little plastered, but you're completely drunk.
JEHAN FROLLO: It pleases you to say that, but it's been proven that Plato had the profile of a hound.
PHOEBUS: Try to listen to me, my good Jehan.
JEHAN FROLLO: Heavens! The Man in Black who followed us has vanished. I tell you, Phoebus, he was the Demon Monk!

PHOEBUS: So be it–it was the Demon Monk then. Listen to me, friend. I gave a rendezvous to the Gypsy girl at eight o'clock, and she's going to come.
JEHAN FROLLO: Go then! You're like the Castle of Dammartin, which laughs in all our faces.
PHOEBUS: Jehan, listen! She's coming here! And I need some money. You heard La Falourdel. She won't give me credit. Mercy, Jehan, haven't we drunk together like brothers? Don't you have any *sous* left?
JEHAN FROLLO (*sententiously*): The awareness of having spent our hours profitably is a true and savory condiment of life.
PHOEBUS (*shaking him*): Will you cut that nonsense! By the Devil, Jehan, do you have any money?
JEHAN FROLLO: Ah! Money! It's money you want! Why didn't you say so sooner? (*fumbling in his pockets*)
PHOEBUS: Ah! My good comrade, you save me! Give it to me, quick! Give it to me, by God, or I'm going to search you myself.
JEHAN FROLLO: For sure, I had ten *sous* a little earlier. But wait, Phoebus, didn't we drink that last coin an hour ago?
PHOEBUS: What! Not a single coin left?
JEHAN FROLLO: None! In fact, I now recall we owe four *sous* at La Pomme d'Eve!
PHOEBUS: Then what the Hell am I wasting my time with you? Go to the Devil, you Student of the Antichrist!
JEHAN FROLLO: By God, yes, I'll be on my way. I'm suffocating in here.

(*He stumbles to the door and bumps into Claude Frollo, enveloped in a long, dark cloak.*)

JEHAN FROLLO: Aie! The Demon Monk! Again! Phoebus, you no longer have your good sense, but I still have mine. Take care of yourself.

(*He leaves, staggering along the way.*)

PHOEBUS (*considering Claude Frollo*): There! Who are you, you grim specter?
CLAUDE FROLLO: A man who wishes to save you.
PHOEBUS: You are bold indeed.
CLAUDE FROLLO: Captain Phoebus de Chateaupers, you are foolhardy.
PHOEBUS: What! You know my name?
CLAUDE FROLLO: I not only know your name, I know that you have a rendezvous here soon.
PHOEBUS: You know that, too?
CLAUDE FROLLO: Yes. And I know the name of the woman who's going to come to this rendezvous...
PHOEBUS: By God! She's the woman that I love, my my Gypsy girl, my dancing flame, my Esmeralda.
CLAUDE FROLLO: Your death.
PHOEBUS (*bursting into peals of laughter*): Ah! You exaggerate, specter! You think that little wisp of a girl is going to kill me?
CLAUDE FROLLO: She will deliver you to the bandits of her tribe.
PHOEBUS: Really! And by what means will she introduce her army? I know this place well. (*pointing to the door to the right*) The room on that side has no entrance but through this door and a garret window. This window gives on the river. Anyway, I fear nothing. I have my sword.
CLAUDE FROLLO: So, you won't renounce this rendezvous?

PHOEBUS: No. Not for all the Devils in Hell!
CLAUDE FROLLO: I tried to help you. You don't wish it. That's fine.
PHOEBUS (*mocking him*): One moment, friend. Would you really like to help me? Truly?
CLAUDE FROLLO: Yes.
PHOEBUS (*laughing*): Well, then, lend me a *sou*!
CLAUDE FROLLO (*after a moment's hesitation*): Here it is. (*Phoebus puts out his hand*) But on one condition.
PHOEBUS: Name it.
CLAUDE FROLLO: Hide me in some corner where I can, if necessary, help you.
PHOEBUS (*aside*): He keeps at it. (*pointing to the door to the right*) Go into that room if you like.
CLAUDE FROLLO: In that room? So be it.
PHOEBUS: Go in quickly. I heard eight rings at Saint-Severin.
CLAUDE FROLLO (*aside*): Perhaps she won't come.
PHOEBUS: I hear someone coming. Go! I will leave the key on your side.

(*La Falourdel enters from the left.*)

LA FALOURDEL: The woman is here. Where's the money?
PHOEBUS (*giving her the* sou): Here, old woman.
LA FALOURDEL: Thanks, Monsieur.

(*She leaves. Phoebus goes to the door on the right.*)

PHOEBUS: The key is on his side, but the bolt is on mine. (*he slips the bolt*)

(*Esmeralda enters left and stops on the threshold, looking confused.*)

PHOEBUS: Come in, come in, my pretty. Shame be you.
ESMERALDA: O, Captain Phoebus, please don't despise me. For I feel what I'm about to do is very wrong.
PHOEBUS: Despise you? Great God! Why should I?
ESMERALDA: For having come here.
PHOEBUS: On that subject, my lovely, you misunderstand me. I ought not to despise you–but hate you.
ESMERALDA: Hate me? Why? What did I do?
PHOEBUS: For your having required so much wooing.
ESMERALDA: Alas, it's true that I'm breaking a vow. I'll never find my true parents now. The amulet will lose its power. But what of it! Oh! Captain Phoebius, I love you so much.
PHOEBUS: So you do love me. (*he throws his arm about Esmeralda's waist*)
ESMERALDA (*gently separating from him*): Captain Phoebus, you're good, you're generous, you're handsome. You saved me, I who am merely a poor lost child of Bohemia. For a long time, I've dreamed of a handsome Captain who would save my life. It was of you that I was dreaming, before I knew you. In my dream, my Captain had a beautiful outfit like yours, a great bearing and a sword. Walk around a bit so I can see you all grand and magnificent.

(*Phoebus prances around smiling.*)

ESMERALDA: How I love hearing the ring of your spurs.
PHOEBUS: Girl!

ESMERALDA (*looking at him adoringly*): How handsome you are. Your name, Phoebus, is a beautiful name. I love your name. I love your sword. Draw your sword, Captain Phoebus, so I can see it.
PHOEBUS (*drawing his sword, smiling*): You're such a child!
ESMERALDA (*taking the sword and kissing it*): You're the sword of a brave man. I love my Captain.
PHOEBUS (*drawing her to the oak bench*): Come, sit beside me and listen to me.
ESMERALDA (*giving him a little slap on his mouth*): No, no, I won't listen to you. Do you love me? I want you to tell me you love me.
PHOEBUS (*half-kneeling and very smoothly, as if he'd said this a million times before*): Do I love you, angel of my life? My body, my blood, my soul–all are yours, all are for you. I love you and I have never loved anyone but you.
ESMERALDA: Is it really true? Haven't you said it to others before?
PHOEBUS: Ah. Perhaps. I don't know–but I certainly never said it like today. (*giving her a kiss*)
ESMERALDA: Oh! This is the moment I should die.
PHOEBUS: Die? What are you saying? It's the moment you should live. Do you love me?
ESMERALDA: Oh! Yes I do!
PHOEBUS: Well, that's all. You will see how I love you, too. You will see how happy we will be (*coming to her and gently removing her ruffle*)
ESMERALDA (*dreamily*): Captain Phoebus, will you instruct me in your religion.
PHOEBUS (*laughing*): My religion! Me instruct you in my religion! Why?
ESMERALDA: So we can get married.

PHOEBUS: Married? Bah! What kind of folly is this, my beautiful temptress? Does one marry one's lover? (*pulling off her ruffle*)
ESMERALDA (*crossing her arms over her breasts*): Captain Phoebus!
PHOEBUS (*fingering her amulet*): What's this?
ESMERALDA: Don't touch it! It's my protector. That's what will enable me to find my family again, if I remain worthy. Oh, please, Captain leave me alone. My poor mother! Where is she? Help me! Leave me alone! (*she pulls away*)
PHOEBUS (*recoiling, in a cold tone*): Ah! That's fine. I see you don't love me at all.
ESMERALDA (*wrapping her arms around his neck*): I don't love you? I don't love my Phoebus? What are you saying? You're tearing my heart! Ah, never mind the amulet! Never mind my mother! So I won't ever know her... I do love you. And you were right, we won't marry. That would bore you. And then, what am I, a poor dancing girl, compared to you? What a joke! A Gypsy from the streets marrying a Captain of the King's Guards! I was crazy! Phoebus, my beloved Phoebus, do you see me? It's me, Esmeralda, look at me. I'm only a little girl whom you can't reject, because she's come here by herself just to love you.

(*Their lips unite in a kiss. After a moment, Claude Frollo climbs through the back window. He comes forward with slow steps behind Phoebus. Suddenly, he stabs him with a dagger.*)

ESMERALDA (*seeing him, screaming*): Ah!
PHOEBUS (*dying*): Ah, you've betrayed me!

(*Phoebus dies. Claude Frollo disappears through the window, jumping into the river.*)

ESMERALDA (*running and calling*): Help! Help! (*she rushes to Phoebus' body*) Phoebus! My Phoebus! He doesn't respond! He's dead!

(*The door is forced open. The Police appear and arrest Esmeralda.*)

SERGEANT: Our Captain! Murdered! Seize this witch!
ESMERALDA: Phoebus! Phoebus! My Phoebus!

CURTAIN

Scene IX
Honorable Amends

The Square or Parvis of Notre-Dame. To the right we can see obliquely the facade of the Cathedral. To the left, there is the Gondelaurier residence, with its overhanging balcony. A crowd stands in the square, surrounding a gibbet. Jehan Frollo, Gringoire and Clopin Trouillefou are huddled together in a corner.

JEHAN FROLLO: Noon! The cart which is bringing our poor Esmeralda to her death is, at this very moment, leaving from La Tournelle! Which of our men is posted there?
CLOPIN TROUILLEFOU: Mathias, with five or six other brave rogues. But there's nothing to be done now. Ah, good Jehan, you have the daring of newcomers who know nothing of the obstacles. We've willingly put our numbers on her route, and told them to be ready for any opportunities, but what can the Court of Miracles do against a swarm of archers?
GRINGOIRE: In broad daylight! At night, at least, there would have been a chance to save her. But, my dear fellow, no one is bold in the sunshine.
JEHAN FROLLO: Still, we can't let our poor sister die a terrible death on that horrible gibbet, without trying to snatch her away. The cart must be entering in the Island of La Cité by now?
CLOPIN TROILLEFOU: Yes. But even though the streets are very narrow, they're being held by armed guards.

JEHAN FROLLO: But what about here, on the Parvis, where she's supposed to make her Honorable Amends? Or at the Place de Greve, where the gibbet is?
CLOPIN TROUILLEFOU: There, we'll be numerous enough.
JEHAN FROLLO: Perhaps then the crowd will join with us?
CLOPIN TROUILLEFOU: I doubt it. It's pretty much accepted that Esmeralda is guilty of the murder of Captain Phoebus.
JEHAN FROLLO (*excitedly*): She can't have done it! She was besotted with him! Why can't they see it?
GRINGOIRE: Alas! Mostly because she was found guilty. (*gesture by Jehan*) Yes, that doesn't mean anything, I agree, but she did admit to the crime.
JEHAN FROLLO: Because they tortured her! That means nothing too! She confessed to anything because they put her to the question.
GRINGOIRE: Then who would the real murderer be?
JEHAN FROLLO: By the Devil's horns, it was that fiend–the Demon Monk. The one I left with Phoebus the night of the murder. I told that repeatedly to the Judge.
GRINGOIRE: For all the good it did! Esmeralda was still found guilty of murder. Your deposition only served to convict her of being a witch and a tool of Satan. And for good measure, they also condemened the little goat, too. Poor Djali. He was beginning to love me as much as his mistress.
CLOPIN TROUILLEFOU: Friend Jehan, there's only one man who could save Esmeralda, that's Captain Phoebus himself–and I believe he's still hovering near death.

JEHAN FROLLO: No, he isn't! I heard they took him to the home of his relatives, the Gondelauriers. But he, too, thinks Esmeralda is guilty.
THE CROWD: There she is! There she is!

(*A tumbrel, surrounded by horsemen dressed in violet tunics with a white cross, arrives onto the square. The Guards beat a passage for it. Esmeralda, in a long white chemise, her hands tied, her hair disheveled, is seated in the cart. The goat is at her feet. The doors of the Cathedral open. Monks in black capes advance, singing death psalms.*)

MONKS (*singing*): Non timebo millia populi circumdantis me: exsurge, Domine; salvum me fac, Deus!

(*The tumbrel is now before the portal. Pierrat Torterue, the Executioner, unties Esmeralda's hands and makes her get down.*)

MONKS (*singing*): De ventre inferi clamavi, et exaudisti vocem meam, et projecisti me in profundum in corde mans, et flumem circumdedit me.

(*Claude Frollo, dressed in a black chasuble with a silver cross, his head covered with a hood, steps and approaches Esmerelda.*)

CLAUDE FROLLO (*loudly*): Girl, are you ready to die?
ESMERALDA: Yes. Phoebus is dead, I only wish to die.
CLAUDE FROLLO: Have you asked God's pardon for all your sins and failings?

(*With a solemn gesture, he waves aside the Executioner and his assistants; they respectfully move back. The Archdeacon then orders Esmeralda to come closer.*)

CLAUDE FROLLO (*low*): Listen, I can still save you.
ESMERALDA (*looking at him*): Who are you?
CLAUDE FROLLO: A man more tortured than you by all your suffering, more aching than you in your agony. A man who has doomed you, but who now can and wants to save you.
ESMERALDA: Ah! It's you! Phoebus' murderer. Go away, specter! Go away or I will denounce you.
CLAUDE FROLLO: They won't believe you. You would only add a scandal to a crime.
ESMERALDA: Oh, wretch! I know you now. All those months, you've pursued me, threatened me, terrified me. What do you have against me? Do you hate me so much?
CLAUDE FROLLO: No! I love you.
ESMERALDA: Some love!
CLAUDE FROLLO: The love of a damned soul! Listen. Tell me only this. Not even that you love me, just that you will let me love you. Say that and I will save you.
ESMERALDA: No! I will not! Never. Thank God that no one can save me now.
CLAUDE FROLLO: I can do it, I promise you. Notre-Dame is a holy place of asylum. I only have to take your hand and draw you inside. The Justice of Man stops on that threshold. Allow me to love you. Permit me to save you. Have pity on me, have pity on yourself!
ESMERALDA: No! I hate you. You killed my Phoebus. I want to join him. Be yours, accursed priest? Never!

CLAUDE FROLLO: Well, then you will never belong to any one. (*loudly again*) I nunc, anima anceps, et sit tibi Deus misenicors!

(*He then turns and runs away, back inside the Cathedral. The Executioner comes to take Esmeralda. He puts a lit yellow wax candle in her hand and makes her kneel before the steps of Notre-Dame. The people kneel too.*)

MONKS (*singing*): Omnes gurgites tui super me transierunt.

(*The Executioner lifts Esmeralda and puts her back in the tumbrel. At that moment, Phoebus, pale and enveloped in a cloak, appears on the Gondelaurier's balcony.*)

ESMERALDA (*seeing Phoebus*): Phoebus! My Phoebus!

(*Phoebus abruptly goes back inside.*)

ESMERALDA: Oh, Phoebus! Do you believe that I am your murderer?

(*She faints. Two of the Executioner's aides put her back in the tumbrel.*)

EXECUTIONER: Now to the Place de Greve! To the gibbet!

(*Suddenly, Quasimodo slides down a rope on the facade of the Cathedral. He rushes the Executioner's aides, knocking them over, and pulls Esmeralda from the tum-*

brel. Holding her high above his head, he carries her across the open doors of Notre-Dame.)

QUASIMODO (*in the threshold, in a powerful voice*): Asylum! Asylum!
JEHAN FROLLO: Asylum!
GRINGOIRE: Asylum!
THE CROWD (*clapping their hands*): Asylum! Asylum! Hurrah!

CURTAIN

Act IV

Scene X
Sanctuary

A vaulted gallery near the rooftop of Notre-Dame. To the right, there is a door, leading to another gallery. Opposite it is a stairway. Against the wall, there is pulpit with a prayer-book on it. A lamp is suspended just above it. Next to it is a small door, leading to a small cubicle. The back of the stage is made up of colonnades.

Quasimodo enters running, carrying Esmeralda He deposits her on a bench made up from a block of stone.

QUASIMODO (*looking at her tenderly*): You're saved! Saved!
ESMERALDA (*shaking her head sadly*): Why did you save me?
QUASIMODO (*looking at her without understanding or hearing her*): You spoke? You want something? Wait.

(*He runs out.*)

ESMERALDA (*alone*): Yes, I will die soon. That will be for the best. And yet, Phoebus, my Phoebus, lives. I saw it, like in a dream! But then, I dreamed that he turned away, fled from me. But how could he believe that such a murderous blow could ever be struck by one who would have given her very life a thousand times to save his? Yet, didn't I confess to it? Didn't I give in, weak woman, to torture? Ah, I ought to have let my fingernails be torn out rather than utter such words...

(*Reenter Quasimodo, leading the goat which runs to his mistress.*)

ESMERALDA: Djali! Ah, it's you my Djali! I'd forgotten you. Oh, you're not an ingrate.
QUASIMODO (*placing before Esmeralda a basket that contains clothes, bread and a bottle*): Here! Here's something to eat; here's a novice's dress that the women of charity have left for you at the Church's door. You can't stay in that criminal's dress. (*he goes to bring everything in and the goat follows him*)
ESMERALDA (*averting her eyes*): Thank you!
QUASIMODO: I frighten you. I am really ugly, huh? Don't look at me, only listen. This is your place of refuge. You can stay here during the day. There's another door leading to the outside gallery. At night, you can wander throughout the whole church. But don't go out–ever! Neither by day nor by night. You would be doomed. They would kill you and I would die. (*he starts to move away*)
ESMERALDA: You're leaving me? Stay.
QUASIMODO (*aside, continuing to move away*): She must be telling me to get out.
ESMERALDA (*going to him and pulling him back by his sleeve*): Stay! I want to speak with you!
QUASIMODO (*incredulous*): You told me to stay?
ESMERALDA (*nodding affirmatively*): Yes.
QUASIMODO: You see... I'm deaf, too.
ESMERALDA: Poor man.
QUASIMODO (*with a melancholy smile*): You think that's all I need, right? Yes, I'm deaf. That's the way I'm

made. Horrible, isn't it? As for you, you're so beautiful. Never have I seen my ugliness as I do now. When I compare myself to you, I really pity myself, poor monster that I am. You must take me for a beast, right? You, you're a beam of sunshine, a rose petal, a bird's song! And me, I'm something terrifying, neither man nor animal, a thing more hammered and more deformed than any stone gargoyle. (*with a heart-rending shout*) Yes, and I am deaf, too! But you can speak to me with gestures, with signs. And I will quickly learn to understand you by the movement of your lips, by your glances.

ESMERALDA: Then, tell me why you saved me.

QUASIMODO (*who watched her attentively as she spoke*): I understood. You asked me why I saved you. You've forgiven the wretch who tried to carry you off one night; a wretch to whom, the very next day, you brought help on the pillory. A drop of water and a little pity. That's more than I can repay with my life. You forgave the wretch. I never forgot.

ESMERALDA: Good and sad Quasimodo–

QUASIMODO (*moving towards the outside gallery*): See, the towers are quite high. A man who falls from them would die before touching the pavement. Whenever you'd like for me to fall for you, you won't even have to say a word, just a glance will suffice.

ESMERALDA (*whose glance has followed Quasimodo's gestures*): Ah!

QUASIMODO: What are you looking at?

ESMERALDA (*arms extended*): Him! Him again! Phoebus!

QUASIMODO: Yes. I see what you see. And I recognize him.

ESMERALDA: My Phoebus!

QUASIMODO: He's the Captain of the Guards who came to your rescue the night I tried to carry you off.
ESMERALDA (*in despair*): Misery! I'm too far away. He can't hear me. The day is ending–he can't see me.
QUASIMODO (*after a silence, with effort*): Would you like me to go fetch him?
ESMERALDA (*with a cry of joy*): Oh! Yes, go, run, run fast! My Captain. Oh! Bring him to me! I will love you!
QUASIMODO (*sadly*): I will bring him to you.
ESMERALDA: Now! Go right away before night falls!
QUASIMODO: First, I've got to light the candle before the Breviary, then I'll go. Meanwhile, you go to that little cell, get changed and eat some food.
ESMERALDA (*going towards the cell*): Yes, I will, but hurry! Hurry!
QUASIMODO: I'm leaving.
ESMERALDA: Thank you!

(*She goes into the cubicle. Quasimodo lights the candle by the prayer-book.*)

QUASIMODO (*alone*): She loves him! Oh! How she loves him! Well, that's how it is. All there is to it is to be good-looking on the outside. Above all.

(*He leaves by the stairway on the left. A moment later, Claude Frollo enters through the opposite gallery.*)

CLAUDE FROLLO: Since I fled, since I tore myself away from that horrible spectacle, what have I done? Where did I go? I don't know. I walked haphazardly, in a fever, a rage, a delirium. Ah, how I suffered! I suffered so much that, at times, I tore out my hair to see if it hadn't turned white. But now what? It's over, she must be dead by now! Hanging from that gibbet on the Place de Greve!

(*The Moon has risen. Esmeralda, dressed in a white dress with a white veil, silently comes out of her cell and walks by the colonnades at the back. Claude Frollo doesn't see her. She disappears behind a pillar.*)

CLAUDE FROLLO: I have reached the bottom of possible sorrow. The human heart can contain only so much pain. When a sponge is bloated, an ocean may pass over it without leaving a single tear in it. Ah, the Breviary. If I could find in that Holy Book some consolation or some encouragement. (*reading*) "And a spirit passed before my face and I heard a breath and my hair stood on end." (*turning away with terror*) Oh, I have made a bad mistake. I grasped a red-hot iron! Come, let's return to my chambers. The poor dead thing is gone. She must be cold by now.

(*He turns towards the moonlit gallery and stops suddenly as he sees Esmeralda advancing slowly in the light, looking toward Heaven.*)

CLAUDE FROLLO (*choking*): God!

(*For each step she takes forward, he takes one back. When she is under the vaulted arch, he falls to his knees, head and arms spread. She does not see him and goes back into her cell.*)

CLAUDE FROLLO (*mechanically*): "A spirit passed before my face, and I heard a breath and my hair stood on end."

(*Suddenly, Gringoire appears in the gallery.*)

GRINGOIRE (*looking about*): Where the Devil am I? I can't find the cell of that Archdeacon.
CLAUDE FROLLO: Gringoire!
GRINGOIRE (*aside, noticing Claude Frollo*): It's him.
CLAUDE FROLLO: What are you doing here? Who are you looking for?
GRINGOIRE: Who? Why, you, Reverend Master. You or Esmeralda.
CLAUDE FROLLO: Esmeralda! What are you saying? Is she still alive?
GRINGOIRE: No doubt. Didn't you know?
CLAUDE FROLLO: Then it wasn't her spirit that I just saw pass before my eyes.
GRINGOIRE: Assuredly.
CLAUDE FROLLO: She was saved! But how? And by whom?
GRINGOIRE: By Quasimodo.
CLAUDE FROLLO: By Quasimodo? Ah, I see. Yes. He's strangely devoted to her now.
GRINGOIRE: He carried her in his arms right into Notre-Dame, and claimed asylum.
CLAUDE FROLLO: Saved! She is saved!
GRINGOIRE: Does that upset you?
CLAUDE FROLLO: No! Oh, no! The torture begins again for me, perhaps, but at least I will bear less guilt.
GRINGOIRE: But we should be careful. I'm really afraid that our poor Esmeralda may not be safe here for very long.
CLAUDE FROLLO: What do you mean?
GRINGOIRE: When Quasimodo so bravely carried her off, Torterue the Executioner was almost as happy as a

dog who has had his bone snatched away. But the King's Prosecutor, Master Jacques Charmolue reassured him. I heard him myself. He said: "Tomorrow, I'll obtain a Special Warrant from the King, and day after, justice will be done!"
CLAUDE FROLLO: Oh. Then it's necessary to make her leave here.
GRINGOIRE: Impossible! The Church is watched and guarded day and night. No one can leave, except those whom they've seen enter. When I presented myself just now, at the Red Gate, asking after you, they warned me to be sure to leave by the same door. All the others were locked.
CLAUDE FROLLO: Ah! Well, there's a way.
GRINGOIRE: What is it?
CLAUDE FROLLO: You will switch clothes with Esmeralda. You will take her clothes, she will take yours.
GRINGOIRE: That's fine for the moment. And then?
CLAUDE FROLLO: And then, she will leave with your clothes, and you will remain with hers.
GRINGOIRE: But then, it's I who will be hanged.
CLAUDE FROLLO: Perhaps, but she will be saved.
GRINGOIRE (*scratching his ear*): Hm. There's an idea I'd never have gotten by myself.
CLAUDE FROLLO: What do you say to it?
GRINGOIRE: I say, Reverend Master, that they won't hang me questionably, they'll hang me positively.
CLAUDE FROLLO: Didn't she save your life at the Court of Miracles? It's a debt you're paying off.
GRINGOIRE: There are many others I'm not paying!
CLAUDE FROLLO: What's wrong with you that you're so attached to life?
GRINGOIRE: Oh, a thousand reasons! The air, the sky, day, night, moonlight, my good friends the vagabonds,

three long poems to finish, what else could I add? And then, I have the good luck of spending all my life with a man of genius–I mean, me! It's very pleasant.
CLAUDE FROLLO: Your head would make a fine horse bell! This life that you find so charming, who saved it for you? To whom do you owe breathing this air, seeing this sky and the ability to fill your empty brain with nonsense and follies? Without her, where would you be? You want her to die, even through you owe her your life, this beautiful, sweet, adorable creature, necesssary to the light of the world? Come, come, show a bit of mercy, Gringoire. Be generous in your turn; it's she who showed you the way.
GRINGOIRE: A moving plea, Reverend Master! That's a queer idea you've got. After all, who knows? Perhaps, they won't hang me. When they find me here, grotesquely dressed in a skirt and a wig, perhaps they'll burst out laughing. And then, if they hang me, well, the rope is a death just like any other! Or to put it better, it's not a death just like any other! It's a death worthy of a philosopher who has vascillated all his life, a death marked by Pyrrhonism and hesitation, half-way between Heaven and Earth, leaving one in suspense. It's a true philosopher's death. Yes, it's magnificent to die as one has lived.
CLAUDE FROLLO: So, you agree then?
GRINGOIRE: Ah! Upon my word, no! Me, to be hanged? It's absurd. I won't.

(*He strides away.*)

CLAUDE FROLLO (*gritting his teeth*): Farewell, then! But be mindful, I will find you again.

GRINGOIRE (*aside*): Ay! I don't want that devil of a man after me. (*returning to Claude Frollo, aloud*) Listen, Reverend Master, Archdeacon, there should be no ill-will between friends. You've taken an interest in this girl–my wife, I mean–that's fine. You've devised a strategem to get her safely out of Notre-Dame. But your way is extremely unpleasant for me, Gringoire. Suppose I find another way? Is it absolutely necessary that I should be hanged for you to be satisfied?
CLAUDE FROLLO: Stop your incessant babble! What is your plan then?
GRINGOIRE (*touching his nose with his finger*): Let me think... Yes, that's it! The Court of Miracles are brave lads. The Tribe of Egypt loves her. They will carry her off at the first word from me. At night, they'll force the doors of the church, and under cover of the disarray that will ensue, they will easily carry her off. I can set it up for tomorrow night.
CLAUDE FROLLO (*aside*): Yes, that way, I'll still have her in my reach. (*aloud*) It's a good plan. When your vagabonds have broken inside, come and find me. I've got the key to the cloister door. I'll let you leave with her through there. It's agreed.
GRINGOIRE: It's agreed. I may be safer with you than with the vagabonds anyway.

(*Quasimodo returns, entering through the staircase.*)

CLAUDE FROLLO: Quasimodo! Come, Gringoire. I don't want to see him. (*pulling Gringoire into the colonnades*)
GRINGOIRE (*aside*): I wish he wouldn't want to see me either.

QUASIMODO (*to himself, sadly*): She told me: “Bring him to me and I will love you.” Since I’m not bringing him, she’s going to hate me.

(*Esmeralda comes out of her cell, running.*)

ESMERALDA: You’re alone!
QUASIMODO (*head lowered*): I wasn’t able to see him.
ESMERALDA: You’ve got to find him. Wait for him! Wait for him all night if that’s what it takes. Go back!
QUASIMODO: I will. Hopefully, I’ll be luckier this time, perhaps.
ESMERALDA: Next time, I’ll go with you.
QUASIMODO (*stopping*): I think I heard you say that next time, you’d go with me? Oh, no! You mustn’t do that! First of all, they will take you again if you leave here. And then, if you find him, you will suffer too much.
ESMERALDA: Why do you say this? Then you did see him!
QUASIMODO: Yes, I did. I wanted to keep the pain to myself. But the truth is that, after having kept me waiting for a long while, he received me.
ESMERALDA: Was he alone?
QUASIMODO: No. He was with a young girl and an older woman. I told him there was someone who wished to speak to him. I understood that the young woman then asked me who it was. I answered that he would soon see. Upon hearing that, she looked at him with scorn. As for him, he spoke to me in a fit of passion. He held the hand of the girl to justify himself to the mother, and in fury, kicked me out.

ESMERALDA: But why talk to him in front of strangers? If he had known it was about me... Ah, when I get to see him alone...
QUASIMODO: My God! Do I have to tell you everything? So be it, then. Listen. I watched the house from the square. When he left, alone, I boldly grabbed the bridle of his horse. And I told him it was a woman who was waiting for him. A woman he loved. And then–oh, you're going to get angry. He answered me with I don't know what insults. It's not my fault. I told him. She's the Gypsy girl you love–Esmeralda! And he kicked me in the chest with his boot. I really beg your indulgence.
ESMERALDA (*joining her hands*): Oh, my Phoebus. It's all right, my friend, you can go now. I thank you.
QUASIMODO: Ah! You don't hold it against me! You are good! But for pity's sake, don't allow yourself to feel too much pain!
ESMERALDA: Yes, yes. Now, go. Leave me alone.
QUASIMODO: Goodbye. Don't be too sad, I beg you! (*starts to leave, then turns*) Ah, wait, if you need me, whistle with this. (*gives her a silver whistle*) I can hear its noise.

(*Quasimodo exits left.*)

ESMERALDA (*thinking herself alone*): Phoebus! My Phoebus! My name, my name alone now horrifies him! Ah! This is reason to despair! But, no! If I see him again, just once, for a single minute, it will only take a word from me, a single glance, to get him back!

(*She turns around and suddenly sees Claude Frollo, who has entered noiselessly from the back.*)

ESMERALDA (*uttering a scream*): Ah, you again! Accursed man!
CLAUDE FROLLO: Do I terrify you so much?
ESMERALDA: Oh, the executioner taunts his victim! It's you who threw me in the abyss! You who committed the crime of which I'm accused! The crime even my Phoebus believe I committed!
CLAUDE FROLLO: Not that name! Don't utter that name! Wretches that we are, it's that name which has ruined us. Oh, young girl, you think yourself miserable, but you don't know what true misfortune is. Oh, to love a woman and be hated by her! To love with all the furor of one's soul, to feel that, for the least of her smiles, you would give your blood, your guts, your fame, your safety, your immortality and eternity, your life and the next! To regret not being a genius, a king, an archangel or a god to place oneself at her feet and become her greatest slave! And to see her fall in love with the shallow uniform of an unworthy soldier! To be there, seething with jealousy and rage, while she squanders treasures of love and beauty on a despicable, stupid braggart!
ESMERALDA: My Phoebus!
CLAUDE FROLLO: Shut up! I beg you! When you say that name, it's as if you were grinding all the fibers of my heart between your teeth. Have mercy! Oh! Say you don't wish to hear me? Ah, the day when a woman rejects such love as mine, I would have thought mountains would have moved by themselves.
ESMERALDA: What have you done with my Phoebus?
CLAUDE FROLLO: Ah. You are merciless.
ESMERALDA: What have you done with my Phoebus?
CLAUDE FROLLO: He is dead.
ESMERALDA: You lie! He still lives. I saw him.
CLAUDE FROLLO: You saw him! Beware.

ESMERALDA: He's alive and it's he alone whom I love.
CLAUDE FROLLO: Shut up!
ESMERALDA: And I belong to him!
CLAUDE FROLLO: To him? Never! Enough of this madness! You will belong to me!

(*He seizes her forcefully and drags her towards the cell.*)

ESMERALDA (*struggling*): Let me go, you murderer!
CLAUDE FROLLO: You're the murderer.
ESMERALDA: Devil!
CLAUDE FROLLO: You're the Devil!
ESMERALDA: Help! Help!

(*They are now close to the cell. Esmeralda uses Quasimodo's whistle. Quasimodo enters, running, knife in hand. He leaps on Claude Frollo and tears Esmeralda away from him, throwing him to the ground.*)

CLAUDE FROLLO (*getting up*): Quasimodo!
QUASIMODO (*recognizing him and recoiling*): Master!
CLAUDE FROLLO: Ah! Wretch! You forget whom you struck!
QUASIMODO: No. Because you're still alive.
CLAUDE FROLLO: Let me pass. Get out of my way!
QUASIMODO (*bending his knee and presenting the knife to him*): You'll have to kill me first.
CLAUDE FROLLO: (*reaching for the knife*) If I must–
ESMERALDA (*snatching the knife and brandishing it at him*): Don't you dare! (*Claude Frollo recoils*) Coward!
CLAUDE FROLLO (*enraged*): Oh! My time will come! And you, misshapen brute... The first time you were

between me and this woman, you served me. This time, you dare defy me!
QUASIMODO (*still on his knees but threateningly*): Beware the third time!

CURTAIN

Act V

Scene XI
The Little Slipper

The Place de Greve, with its grim gibbet. To the right, in a cut-out fashion, we see the interior of La Sachette's cell in the Roland Tower and the wall with the small garret window shut with crossed bars. We hear the distant clamor of the Tocsin. It is night, but dawn is coming by degrees.

SACHETTE (*lying on straw bed, a stone serving as her pillow*): O my daughter, my daughter! My poor dear child! I will never see you again. It's as if it had happened only yesterday. My God! My God! Taking her away from me so quickly it would have been better not to give her to me. Ah, wretch that I am to have gone out that day! O Lord, O Lord! To take her away from me that way, you mustn't have seen me with her when I warmed her up so happily by my fire. When she laughed at me when I held her in my arms. When I raised her little feet to my lips. God, you would have had pity on me. You would not have separated me from the only joy that remained in my heart. Was I such a wretched creature, Lord, that you could not look at me before condemning me? Alas, alas, here's her little slipper. But where is her foot? Where is the child? My daughter, what have they done to you, those vampires from Egypt! Lord, please, return her to me. My knees are raw from 15 years of praying to you. My God, isn't that enough?

Return her to me for one hour, one day, one minute. One minute, Lord, then hurl me down to Hell for all eternity, if that is your wish. Can you condemn a poor mother to 15 years of torture? Good Virgin Mary in Heaven! My Baby Jesus! The Gypsies took her from me, stole her from me. They ate her on their hearth. Ah, my daughter, my daughter! I must have my daughter. What good is it to me if she is in paradise? I don't want an angel, I want my child. I am a lioness, I want my cub! So much the worse if I blaspheme! As for me, I am nothing but a vile sinner! But my daughter is making me pious! I was full of religion for the love of her and through her smile, I saw you, my God, like an opening in Heaven. Oh, let me just once, just once more, a single time, put this slipper on her little foot and I will die, good Virgin, and bless you. Ah, 15 years. Can it be true? I will never see her again. Not even in Heaven! For as for me, I'm not headed there. Oh, what despair! This is her slipper and that's all I have left of her!

(*Enter from the right Clopin Trouillefou, Chanteprune, Bellevigne and five or six vagabonds. They bear the body of Jehan Frollo.*)

CLOPIN TROUILLEFOU: Let's stop and catch our breath a minute. (*to Bellevigne*) You, run and see if our passage through the Rue de la Mortellerie is still free.

(*Chanteprune leaves.*)

CLOPIN TROUILLEFOU: Poor Jehan. Is he still breathing?
CHANTEPRUNE: No, Sire, he is dead.

CLOPIN TROUILLEFOU: Thrown by Quasimodo from the top of the great gallery of Notre-Dame. Ah, that Quasimodo! Why did he defend the church against our assault with his huge stones and his melted lead? Gringoire said that he, like us, only sought to save Esmeralda?
CHANTEPRUNE: He wasn't warned of our plan. He didn't understand. He's deaf and he didn't hear.

(*Bellevigne returns.*)

BELLEVIGNE: The passage is free.
CLOPIN TROUILLEFOU: Quick! Quick! I hear Captain Phoebus' guards coming. Hurry!

(*They leave by the left, carrying Jehan's body. Gringoire enters in the corner, leading Esmeralda. Behind them is Claude Frollo, wrapped in his black monk cloak.*)

GRINGOIRE (*in a low voice to Claude Frollo*): Come, come, Reverend Master. I hear the guards. But you have the power to lift their barriers in the streets. All the same, I think you were wrong to not tell Quasimodo of our plan. Who was that poor devil your bell-ringer threw over the rampart of the gallery?
CLAUDE FROLLO (*shivering*): I don't know and I don't care. Go now, go. Return to the barge.
ESMERALDA: Gringoire! Are you leaving us?
GRINGOIRE: I'll be back. I'm going to the barge to get Djali.
ESMERALDA: But who are you leaving me with?
GRINGOIRE: Oh. With someone who's very devoted to you, don't worry.

(*He leaves quickly.*)

ESMERALDA (*calling after him*): Gringoire! Don't leave! Where are you? (*suddenly noticing Claude Frollo*) Who are you? (*Frollo raises his hood*) Oh no! The Devil!
CLAUDE FROLLO: This is the Place de la Greve. There is the gibbet. We've reached the end. Fate has delivered us to each other. I shall decide your life and you, my soul. Don't speak to me of your Phoebus! If you speak his name, I don't know what I will do, but it will be terrible. There's a Special Warrant ordering me to deliver you to the scaffold. I just received it. The King's Guards are after you. Listen to them!
SHOUTS (*in the distance*): The Gypsy girl! Where is the Gypsy girl?
CLAUDE FROLLO: I can save you right now. I've planned everything. It shall be as you wish. Whatever you wish, I can do. (*violently interrupting himself*) No, that's not enough. (*taking her left hand and pointing her to the gibbet*) The gibbet, you see it. Choose between us.
ESMERALDA (*going to the gibbet*): It terrifies me less than you.
CLAUDE FROLLO: You do hate me so much then! Why, you cannot even raise your eyes to look at me. (*Esmeralda starts to speak*) No, don't speak to me of this Phoebus! Look, I will tear not just words, but my heart and my very guts from my breast to tell you that I love you. And yet it all seems so futile. You have nothing in your soul but tenderness and mercy for all–but none for me. You shine with the most radiant love. Yet, for me and me alone, you are an evil that must be extinguished. O, please, give me a word of kindness. Say a word, only a word!

ESMERALDA: I belong to my Phoebus. It's Phoebus who is handsome, it's Phoebus whom I love!
CLAUDE FROLLO (*with a terrible scream*): Ah!

(*He grabs Esmeralda and drags her towards the cell.*)

CLAUDE FROLLO: Die then!
ESMERALDA (*with terror*): Where are you taking me?
CLAUDE FROLLO: One last time. Will you be mine?
ESMERALDA: No.
CLAUDE FROLLO: La Sachette!
SACHETTE (*standing up*): What do you want with me?
CLAUDE FROLLO: Here's a Gypsy. Avenge yourself.
SACHETTE (*grabbing Esmeralda's hand through the bars*): Ha! The Gypsy girl.
CLAUDE FROLLO: Hold her tight. Don't let her go. I am going to find the King's Guards. You will see her hang.
SACHETTE (*with a mad laugh*): Ha! Ha! Ha! Daughter of Gypsies. You are going to hang.
ESMERALDA: What have I done to you?
SACHETTE: What have you done to me? What did you do to me, Gypsy girl? Listen! I had a daughter. Me! A pretty young girl. Well, Gypsy girl, your people took my child away from me. They stole her from me! That's what you did to me!
ESMERALDA: But I wasn't born then.
SACHETTE: Oh, yes, you were! My daughter was around your age. Do you have a heart? Imagine a baby playing, nursing, sleeping–so innocent. Well, that's what your people took from me. The poor child! While she slept! And if they had awakened her when they took her, it wouldn't have done any good, for I wasn't there. Ah,

you Gypsies devoured my child. Now come see yours hang! Ha! Ha! Ha!
ESMERALDA (*on her knees, terrified*): Madame! Madame! Have mercy! The guards are coming. I never did anything to you. Do you want me to die in this horrible manner before your eyes? Let me go. Please release me! Mercy. I don't want to die like that.
SACHETTE: Give me back my child.
ESMERALDA: Mercy!
SACHETTE: Give me back my child.
ESMERALDA: Release me in the name of Heaven.
SACHETTE: Give me back my child!
ESMERALDA: Alas, you seek your child. And me, I seek my parents.
SACHETTE: Return her to me. You don't know where she is? Well then, be prepared to die! Here, let me show you... This is her slipper; all that remains of her. Do you know where is its twin? If you do, tell me and I will let you go and find her, even to the ends of the Earth. On my knees, I so swear!
ESMERALDA (*shivering*): That slipper! Show it to me again. God! O God! (*with her free hand, she opens the bag around her neck*)
SACHETTE: Go! Go! Search your Devil's amulet.
ESMERALDA (*pulling a little identical slipper from the sack*) I have its twin!
SACHETTE: My daughter?
ESMERALDA: My Mother!
SACHETTE: Your hand! Give me your hand! (*throwing herself on Esmeralda's hand, kissing it, weeping*) Oh, the wall. Oh, to see her and not hug her! Wait!

(*She runs to the stone which served as her pillow and digs it up with her hands.*)

SACHETTE: Move away!

(*She hurls the stone at the bars, which break loose. Then she pulls herself through the window.*)

SACHETTE: Come! Come! Now I pull you back from the abyss.

(*Grabbing Esmeralda, she pulls her into the cell.*)

SACHETTE: My daughter! My daughter! I have my daughter back! Come here everybody! Is there anyone here to see that I have my daughter back? Lord God, how beautiful she is. You made me wait 15 years, my good God. But it was to make her beautiful for me. It's really you. So that's why my heart jumped every time you passed. I mistook it for hate. Oh, forgive me! You thought me bad, didn't you? But now I love you. Your pendant around your neck. Have you always had it? Let's see. She still has it. Oh, how beautiful you are. It's I who made those big eyes there. Oh, I love you so much. Now I no longer care about the other mothers who have their own children. They can come and look at mine now! Marvel at her neck, her eyes, her hair, her hands. All my beauty is gone, but hers is here. My God! My God! Who would have believed it? I have my daughter back.
ESMERALDA: Oh my mother. The Gypsy women told me. There was a good woman of our tribe who died last year and who always took care of me, like a nurse. It was she who put this bag around my neck. She always told me: "Little one, guard this carefully. It's a treasure.

It will enable you to find your mother someday." She predicted it, the old Gypsy woman.
SACHETTE: You say that so sweetly. My God! What a pretty voice you have. When you speak, it's like music, Ah, my Lord God, I've found my daughter again. Nothing can hurt me anymore for I am suffused with joy.

(*Outside, we hear the noise of galloping horses.*)

ESMERALDA: Ah! The King's Guards! Save me! Save me, my mother. They're coming.
SACHETTE: Oh, Heavens! I'd forgotten! They're after you. What did you do?
ESMERALDA: I don't know, but I've been condemned to death.
SACHETTE: To death! To death!
ESMERALDA: Yes, Mother. They intend to hang me. They're coming to take me. That gibbet is for me. Save me! Save me! They're coming.
SACHETTE: Oh! No, it's a nightmare you're telling me. I lost you for 15 years, and when I find you again, it lasts only a minute. No, no, God! That thing is not possible.
A VOICE (*outside*): This way, Messire Provost. The Archdeacon said we would find her at the cell of the Recluse.
SACHETTE (*with a scream of despair*): Escape, my child! Everything's coming back to me! You're right. It's your death. Save yourself.

(*Tristan l'Hermite, several Guards and the Torterue the Executioner appear.*)

SAQCHETTE (*low*): Stay here. Don't breathe. Hide in the corner.

(*Esmeralda hides, squatting in a corner of the wall as Sachette runs to the window.*)

TRISTAN L'HERMITE: Old woman! We seek a witch to hang her. We were told you had her prisoner.
SACHETTE: I don't know what you mean.
TRISTAN L'HERMITE: Don't lie to me! I'm the Provost of the Guard. The Archdeacon gave you a witch to watch. What did you do with her?
SACHETTE: If you speak of the young girl that was holding my hands before, she bit me and I had to let her go. She ran away. That's all I know. Now, leave me alone.
TRISTAN L'HERMITE: She ran away! Which way did she go?
SACHETTE: By the Rue du Mouton, I think.
TRISTAN L'HERMITE: Impossible. It's still fenced off.
SACHETTE: Ah! Well, she must have fled by the river then.
TRISTAN L'HERMITE: There's no boat there. God's head, old woman, you're lying! I feel like letting this witch go and taking you instead. A quarter of an hour on Master Torterue's rack will draw the truth from your throat. You're coming with us.
SACHETTE (*eagerly*): As you wish, Messire. Yes, yes. The rack, indeed. I obey. Take me there at once. Let's go! (*low to Esmeralda*) Meanwhile, you run away.
TRISTAN L'HERMITE (*laughing*): God's blood! What an appetite for the rack! Come on, men, she really is as crazy as they say. (*looking towards the square*) Ah! I see the rest of my men have arrived. They'll help us find that

girl. I won't rest until that Gypsy witch dances at the end of a rope.

(*He leaves with the Guards.*)

SACHETTE (*turning, radiantly to her daughter*): Saved! You're saved!
VOICE OF PHOEBUS (*in the square*): No, Provost, no! That's not my business, hanging witches. I'm a soldier.

(*Esmeralda, at Phoebus' first word, runs to the window.*)

ESMERALDA: Phoebus! Help me, my Phoebus!
SACHETTE (*pulling her violently back*): Foolish girl! Stay back!

(*She replaces the bars with her two hands, leaning on the stone like claws. But it's too late: the Provost and his men stride back.*)

TRISTAN L'HERMITE: Ah! Ah! Here's your witch, Master Torterue. Take her!
EXECUTIONER: Which one, Provost?
TRISTAN L'HERMITE: The young one.
EXECUTIONER (*approaching the window*): Madame–
SACHETTE (*in an angry voice*): What do you want?
EXECUTIONER: Not you. The other one.
SACHETTE: What other one?
EXECUTIONER: The girl.
SACHETTE: There's no one here! No one! No one!
EXECUTIONER: Come! You know quite well the girl's in here with you! Let me take her. I mean you no harm.
SACHETTE (*with a strange sneer*): Ah! You mean me no harm! Me!

TRISTAN L'HERMITE: Come on, Master Torterue! Hurry up!
EXECUTIONER: Er, Messire, how do I enter?
TRISTAN L'HERMITE: Through the door.
EXECUTIONER: There isn't any.
TRISTAN L'HERMITE: Through the window then.
EXECUTIONER: It's too narrow.
TRISTAN L'HERMITE: Let the men enlarge it.

(*Two Guards rush out.*)

TRISTAN L'HERMITE: But, God's Head, what's wrong with you, old woman? Why prevent this witch from being hanged as the King ordered?
SACHETTE (*hysterical*): What's wrong with me? She's my daughter!
TRISTAN L'HERMITE (*shivering despite himself*): Ah... (*after a pause*) I'm sorry for it, truly I am, but the King's orders must be obeyed. Break down the wall, men!

(*The two men return with picks and axes and begin to remove the stones next to the window.*)

SACHETTE: Oh! This is too deadful! You're worse than brigands! Are you really going to take my daughter away? Cowards, butchers, murderers.

(*Two large stones are finally removed. La Sachette, arms extended, blocks the opening with her body.*)

SACHETTE: Help! Help!
TRISTAN L'HERMITE: Now take the girl.

SACHETTE (*formidable*): Over my dead body! A thousand curses upon whom who seizes my daughter!

(*The Guards back away.*)

TRISTAN L'HERMITE: Come on! My men, afraid of an old woman! Let's be done with this. (*threateningly*) Or there'll be Hell to pay...

(*Three men advance resolutely.*)

SACHETTE (*with a terrible scream*): Ah! Wait!

(*She rushes out of the cell and falls at the Provost's feet.*)

SACHETTE: Messire! You don't know her story. She's no witch. She's my daughter that I lost. Yes, the Gypsies took her and hid her from me for 15 years. I thought she was dead. Imagine, my good friends, that I thought she was dead! I cried so much that the Good Lord heard me. He returned my daughter to me. You can't take her away from me. Do what you will with me, I won't resist. But she, she's but a child. Give her time to see the Sun. You're so good, all of you! You didn't know that she is my daughter. Now, you do. Oh, Messire, you have a mother. In her name, I implore you: leave me my child. The King! You mentioned the King? It won't give him any joy to kill my little daughter. And besides, she's my daughter, not the King's, not yours. Oh, say the word and we'll leave together and live in exile, just two women, mother and daughter. Let us go, I beg you. You can't take my darling little girl from me, you just can't. She's my child! My child! My child!

TRISTAN L'HERMITE (*low to the Executioner*): Finish up quickly!

(*The Guards take a step toward Esmeralda, who remains shivering at the entrance of the cell. She utters a scream and rushes into her mother's arms.*)

ESMERALDA: Mother! Mother! They're going to take me away. Protect me!
SACHETTE (*clasping her in her arms and covering her with kisses*): Yes, my love, yes, I'll protect you.
TRISTAN THE HERMITE (*to the Executioner*): Finish, I tell you.

(*The Executioner grabs Esmeralda under the shoulders.*)

ESMERALDA: No! No! Please! Mother! Please!

(*The Executioner drags Esmeralda, but La Sachette still clings to her. One of the Guards, with some effort, manages to tear the Old Woman away. But she escapes and rushes Torterue and bites his hand. He lets out a scream and slaps her violently. She reels back, twists around and falls heavily on the pavement.*)

SACHETTE: Ah.

(*She remains motionless–dead. The Executioner continues to carry off Esmeralda, who has fainted.*)

CURTAIN

Scene XII
The Northern Tower of Notre-Dame

A three-leveled stage representing a cut-out of the top levels of the Northern Tower of Notre-Dame. The lower level is a landing between two flight of stairs, with a wooden door on each side, one going down, the other up. The second level, or landing, is the same, except with the clockwork machinery of the Bell Tower. The third, or top level, is the summit of the Tower. There is an openwork balustrade and a bird's eye view of Paris and the river Seine below.

(*Claude Frollo enters the lower level left, from the door leading down; he looks haggard.*)

CLAUDE FROLLO: Where to flee from that horrible spectacle?

(*An angry Quasimodo enters soon after.*)

CLAUDE FROLLO: Leave me! One last time, I order you to leave me! Why did you follow me since the Place de Greve? You look like a wild beast!
QUASIMODO: A wild beast indeed. Who has always been my only Master? You! And what have you taught me? Violence, crime. To kill what you hate. To kill what you love. So I'm going to kill you. Do you still have the knife with which you struck the Captain? Defend yourself then. If not, I will kill you with the knife which you used against me.

(*He rushes Claude Frollo, knife in hand. The Archdeacon tries to run towards the door through which he entered, but Quasimodo easily bars his way.*)

CLAUDE FROLLO: Help!
QUASIMODO: You won't escape so easily.

(*The pursuit begins. Claude Frollo then runs towards the door to his right, leading upstairs, and takes it. Quasimodo follows.*

When he reaches the second level, he tries to lock the wooden door which similarly separates the stairway from the landing. But Quasimodo holds it back. There is a fierce struggle between the two as each pushes the door from his side. Quasimodo finally proves the stronger and erupts on the second landing. Again, knife in hand, he goes after Claude.)

CLAUDE FROLLO: Murderer! You're going to be a murderer!
QUASIMODO: I already am. Because of you, I murdered your very own brother last night. It was him I threw to his death from this very Tower!
CLAUDE FROLLO: Help! Help!

(*Running from Quasimodo, Frollo manages to open the other door leading to the top of the Tower. As Quasimodo strikes, he avoids the blow, slips through the door and manages to lock it behind him.*)

QUASIMODO (*uttering a cry of rage*): Damn!

(*He puts his massive shoulder to the door and it creaks under his power, but doesn't give way. Quasimodo then grasps it with both hands and succeeds in raising it from its hinges. He then rushes after Claude Frollo. Meanwhile, the Archdeacon has arrived breathlessly on the platform.*)

CLAUDE FROLLO: I'm saved. That oak door is between him and me. From here, I can call for help. (*leaning over*) Help! Help. Oh, help will surely come.

(*Quasimodo rushes in.*)

QUASIMODO: Not in time to avoid punishment. (*showing him a point in the distance*) From here, you can see the Place de Greve. From here, you can behold your latest crime. That sweet and angelic creature now hangs from that grim gibbet. Here, I no longer need that knife to render justice.

(*Quasimodo, tossing his knife down below the balustrade, slowly advances towards Claude Frollo.*)

CLAUDE FROLLO: Help! Help! Help!

(*The Archdeacon tries to take refuge behind the corner turret. Quasimodo finds him there and forces him to come onto the sill, then seizes him by the legs and throws him over the balustrade.*

Claude Frollo's gown gets hooked on a gargoyle. The Archdeacon clutches at it with both hands. But, little by little, the gargoyle bends and gives way under his weight. He utters a scream and falls.)

QUASIMODO (*looking at the square and the Place de Greve*): Oh! Everything I loved!

FINAL CURTAIN

The Passion of Frankenstein

by

Frank J. Morlock

Statement by Alexandre Dumas, fils*:*

I found several papers after my father's death which were very disturbing. He had hidden them in various places, and some consisted merely of notes. This is one I have pieced together from letters and notes

As is well known, in the year 1831, my father was a close friend of Victor Hugo's. Rivalries that later estranged them had not yet emerged. Hugo had just written Notre-Dame de Paris *to considerable critical success. Not long after the publication of that work, which gave the world Esmeralda and Quasimodo, my father wrote of a conversation that took place between himself and Hugo:*

Victor came to me last night, highly agitated.

"What's wrong, Victor? You seem to be shaking?" I asked.

"I've had a terrible experience, Alexandre," he replied. "I wish you had been with me."

"What on Earth is wrong? You look as if you've seen a ghost."

"I don't think a ghost would have frightened me so much."

"Well, what has happened?"

Hugo prowled around the room and kept going up to the fireplace to warm himself. He seemed unwilling to tell me at first, so, like a good friend, I waited for him to calm down and collect himself. Still, he hesitated.

"You're going to think I'm having hallucinations," he said.

"I promise I won't."

"Promise on our friendship that you will never reveal this to anyone."

"I promise. Now tell me what happened."

"I was taking a stroll by the Seine with a vague notion of paying you a visit when I was accosted quite suddenly by–a–a monster."

"A monster? What kind of monster?" I asked.

"A sort of giant. Considerably larger than you, Alexandre."

"Did he threaten you?"

"No, he was very respectful, which made it all the more eerie. He came out of the shadows, huge, awkward, not really looking as though he were human. He wore peasant's clothes and had a heavy hat pulled down over his face. I'm not sure how large he was exactly, but he seemed immense, and he radiated enormous physical strength. But he was awkward. Uncoordinated. He pulled off his hat and made something like a bow to me...

" 'Mr. Victor Hugo?' he inquired.

" 'Yes,' I replied.

" 'The author of *Notre-Dame de Paris*?'

" 'Yes.'

" 'Which was published on March 16 of this year?'

" 'Yes.'

" 'You cannot know how enthused I am for your book.'

" 'Thank you.'

" 'I loved that book.'

" 'Thank you again.'

" 'I mean to say, I loved Quasimodo.'

“ ‘Again, I’m much obliged to you.’

“ ‘I’d–I’d like to meet him!

“ ‘What?’

“ ‘I want to meet Quasimodo.’

“ ‘I’m afraid that’s impossible.’ ”

“Your admirer, or rather Quasimodo’s admirer, seems rather original, Victor,” I said, interrupting him.

“Mad, I think,” he agreed. “When I said it was impossible, he began to shake, all seven or eight feet of him. And he became very agitated.

“ ‘Why is it impossible, sir? I *must* see him,’ he begged me.

“ ‘But Quasimodo is a character of my imagination,’ I protested. ‘He’s not a real person. And if he were a real person, he’d be over 300 years old.’

“ ‘I am sure Quasimodo is a real person.’

“ ‘Well, I’m sure he’s not.’

“ ‘I insist on meeting him.’

“ ‘But I’ve just told you he’s a creature of my imagination–’

“ ‘No!’

“ ‘Are you mad?’

“ ‘Quasimodo is a real person, and he’s exactly like me. He must be real.’

“ ‘I assure you...’

“ ‘You must have based him on a real person.’

“ ‘Perhaps vaguely from my research. But that person, if indeed he had a real existence, died in 1481.’

“ ‘Then you must turn back time so I can meet him.’

“ ‘Sir, not even God can turn back time as you put it. I bid you good night.’

“I thought he was going to attack me, so violent were the emotions that the Monster seemed to be experiencing. But suddenly, he controlled himself, put his hat back over his head and begged me to pardon him. He vanished into the shadows."

We discussed it for a while, but we were unable to make any sense of it. Who was this "Monster?" Why did he have such feelings for a hunchback who lived in a belltower of Notre-Dame several hundred years ago. I asked Victor to let me walk him home. He agreed. It was years before we mentioned the incident again.

Another fragment by my father:

While I was working on my play *Urbain Grandier*, in which I decribe the phenomenon of "channeling" and "far sensing," I decided to see if I could channel events myself. I wasn't having much success...

Then, I remembered the incident that Hugo had described to me and decided to see if I could visualize the monster. But that, too, didn't work. Later, it occurred to me that it all had something to do with Notre-Dame and Quasimodo. So I searched my library and found my copy of *Notre-Dame de Paris*. I skipped through it, focusing on incidents where Quasimodo appears. First, as the King of Fools, later, being whipped on the gallows. By the time I reached the final scene where Quasimodo is chasing Claude Frollo across the top of Notre-Dame and then stopping to watch Esmeralda being hanged on the Place de Grève, it was getting rather late at night and I had consumed quite a bit of wine, so it is small wonder if I was dreaming at this point.

But, suddenly, my hair stood straight on end. I felt I was *there*, although invisible, atop Notre-Dame, watching with Quasimodo as Esmeralda was being hanged in the distance.

I read and reread that last paragraph, then continued:

Quasimodo raised his eye to stare at the Gypsy girl whose body he could see suspended on the gibbet, quivering in the distance, in the last struggles of death. He looked down at the Archbishop sprawled at the bottom of the tower, no longer having a human form. With a sob that shook his deep chest, he cried:

"Oh, all that I ever loved."

Suddenly, I felt not only the pain of Quasimodo, but also the empathy that the huge creature felt when he read this. Victor's novel basically ended there, but there was more... I was there, beside Quasimodo... I sensed that he was ready to jump. Suddenly, from nowhere, appeared a man dressed in armor, who placed his hand on Quasimodo's shoulder and said in voice that must be obeyed:

"Don't!"

Quasimodo shuddered and turned around, but was still clinging to his idea. He struggled against the powerful hand on his shoulder that held him back.

"No, I said," said the other.

"Esmeralda is dead, hanging like a pigeon," said Quasimodo. "I want to die."

"Esmeralda will live if you will listen to me."

"Esmeralda will live?"

"Yes."

"Who are you?"

"Someone who can help you, Quasimodo."

"You can save Esmeralda?"

"Yes, I can save Esmeralda."

"Then I will do whatever you say."

"Then come with me to fetch her."

"Are you the Devil?"

"No, but I've been called by that name."

"I don't care if you are, if you will save Esmeralda. What is your name?"

"I am Dracula."

Placing his arms around Quasimodo, the man who had just called himself Dracula suddenly began to rise into the air; he seemed to sprout huge wings from beneath a military cape. Then, beating his wings like a kite, he flew straight from Notre-Dame to the Place de Grève, where Esmeralda still dangled lifelessly from the gibbet.

The crowd looked up thunderstruck to see Quasimodo in the arms of a knight hovering over the scaffold. Dracula hissed "Begone!" to the men and women, who seemed to be forced back by the power of his breath, which was like a huge gust of wind.

"Can you cut her down?" he asked Quasimodo.

"Yes, Lord."

"Do so."

Dracula stood over Esmeralda's lifeless body. He gently placed his hands on her neck and gave it a sudden twist.

"Not a moment too soon," he whispered.

Esmeralda opened her eyes.

"She's alive," screamed Quasimodo. "She's alive!"

The executioner having got his wits together, he rushed up, brandishing his axe.

"There'll be no rescues, here," he shouted.

Two sergeants-at arms seconded his efforts. Quasimodo, letting out a scream of rage, lunged straight at the executioner, who blanched before the Hunchback's savage attack.

Dracula drew his sword and effortlessly dispatched the two armed soldiers.

"Quasimodo, pick up the girl and I will fly you both off," he commanded.

The Hunchback obeyed unquestioningly. A moment later, they were gone.

And I woke suddenly in a cold sweat.

I decided it was a dream. I didn't tell Hugo about it for some time. When I did, Victor said that, if my vision were true, then Dracula, who was a vampire, had turned both Esmeralda and Quasimodo into creatures of the night. He shook his head and refused to say more. Of course, that's pure nonsense.

Still, all that did not explain the monster who had accosted him years ago.

The next thing I found in my father's file was a very strange letter addressed to Victor Hugo. It bore no date but apparently was written some time after Hugo's meeting with the "Monster." The scrawl was crude and difficult to decipher.

Dear Monsieur Hugo,

I am taking the liberty of writing to you. I think that when I first accosted you personally I–my presence is a little disconcerting to most people–which is why I have lived in retreat for many years. You may remember the rather large man who was very interested in Quasimodo? I regret that I was very emotional when I asked you to help me. I apologize very sincerely for my rudeness, but if you knew my story you would understand that I have had little opportunity to obtain the trappings of civilization. It's for that reason that I am writing you, because I cannot discuss this matter without becoming very emotional.

I left you with the conviction that, somehow, Quasimodo was a real person. You, of course, denied that and considered that he was completely a child of your imagination–a proposition with which my entire soul could not agree. But what to do? I wanted to go back in time to save Quasimodo and, as I understand now, you thought I was completely crazy.

I thought about it for a long time. Was there such a thing as an ability to go back in time? I realized how strange I must sound to you. You went back using your imagination. But could one really go? The idea haunted me. Modern science is so powerful. It was able to create me–a man-made man. Unfortunately, I turned out to be a creature repulsive to all men–let's not talk about that. I decided to consult with some very learned men.

I went to see–(*here the manuscript was erased and the name deliberately rubbed out–A.D.* fils.) and this is how our conversation went:

" 'But you did not make me,' I said, after he correctly identified my nature.

" 'Didn't I?' he said.

" 'No. It was your friend and colleague, Victor Frankenstein.'

" 'Ah, yes. I remember him. Been dead a long time. He was experimenting with artificial life...'

" 'I am the result of that experiment.'

" 'Not bad really, for a first effort.'

" 'I am a monster.'

" 'You've improved considerably, I believe. At least, compared to the initial reports I heard.'

" 'I've had an education.'

" 'Yes, you're something of an autodidact.'

" 'Have you ever read *Notre-Dame de Paris* by Victor Hugo?'

" 'No, I'm not much for fiction.'

" 'There's a character in that book–'

" 'Yes ?'

" 'His name is Quasimodo.'

" 'And?'

" 'He was a hunchback. An outcast. I feel a great sympathy for him.'

" 'Why?'

" 'Because he was a Monster–just like me.'

" 'Ah!'

" 'But he had a good heart. A very good heart. He loved this Gypsy girl...'

" 'Well, I'm glad you've found someone to sympathize with–even if he's only a character in a book. It proves your essential humanity.'

" 'But I think he was real.'

" 'Real?'

" 'Yes.'

" 'How can that be?'

" 'I don't know but I'm convinced of it.'

" 'It's a work of fiction, right?'

" 'Yes, set in 1481. I want you to send me back in time so I can save him.'

" 'But I cannot do that.'

" 'Why not?'

" 'Because no one can do that. It's impossible.' "

I admit I was becoming very agitated at this point. I got up and started screaming:

" 'Why impossible? You, too, have created life! If you can do that, you can turn back time. You can do whatever you please.'

" 'Sir, I am not a magician. Modern science is helpless to do this.' "

I began to shake him. But he persisted.

“ ‘What you need is a Magician, a Wizard–someone like Faustus or Balsamo, or the Comte de Saint Germain.’ ”

I swear I did not intend to harm him, but I became so agitated and I’m so strong, you see, that I shook him like a rag doll. And after a while I noticed that he was dead. I was very upset. Someday, I must learn to control my emotions...

I consulted several other scientists, but they all told me the same thing. The idea of time travel was interesting but far beyond our current science. One fellow said it might be possible, but several centuries of work would be required. But they all said what I needed was a necromancer, a magician.

Finally, I declared myself defeated. Science held no hopes for me. I decided to follow their advice and seek out a wizard. But where does one find a wizard these days?

It turned out to be very easy. I was walking through the streets of Paris, quite near Notre-Dame, as a matter of fact, when I saw a sign in a window: “*Tarot Readings. Learn the Future from the Celebrated Doctor Festus, Recently Returned from Germany where he astounded the Court of Weimar. Simple reading: 5 francs. Special reading: 10 francs.*”

So I went in.

“ ‘I am seeking Doctor Faustus,’ I said.

“ ‘I’m Doctor Festus,’ replied the little man behind the counter.

“ ‘Are you the same person?’

“ ‘Some people think so.’

“ ‘And can you travel through time?’

“ ‘They say I can.’

“ ‘And what do you say?’

“ ‘I refuse to say unless I’m well paid.’

“ ‘You want money?’

“ ‘Yes.’

“ ‘A lot?’

“ ‘I’m reasonable.’

“ ‘Will this do?’ I asked, spreading a few hundred francs before him.

“ ‘Yes, that will do very nicely.’

He reached to take the coins, but I placed my hand on the money.

“ ‘I’m glad to give you the money–if you can really take me back in time. But don’t play games with me–Doctor Faustus.’

“ ‘Festus. I won’t play games with you. But I will need a little time to prepare.’

“ ‘They say that you are a magician?’

“ ‘There are rumors to that effect.’

“ ‘Are you any good at it?’

“ ‘I’m the best in the world.’

“ ‘Then send me back to the year 1481.’

“ ‘1481? Why, for Heaven’s sake ? Nothing much going on then as I recall.’

“ ‘You were there?’

“ ‘Of course, I was there.’

“ ‘That was the year that Quasimodo...’

“ ‘Quasimodo–who’s he?’

“ ‘A character in a novel.’

“ ‘Umm?’

“ ‘But I’m sure he was real–’

“ ‘And you want to go back in time?’

“ ‘To–to meet him.’

“ ‘Where was he living?’

“ ‘In Paris. He was the bellringer of Notre-Dame.’

“ ‘Well, that does make things a bit easier–we don’t have far to travel in space.’

“ ‘How will you do it?’

“ ‘The means are my concern. Here, take your money. Come back tomorrow night and I will be prepared. How long do you intend to stay?’

“ ‘If all goes well only a few hours. I just have to save him.’

“ ‘Hmm. I’d better accompany you.You’ll need a guide.’ ”

So I am writing this to you, Monsieur Hugo, before I leave for 1481. You cannot imagine the joy and anticipation I am experiencing. If I return successfully, you will hear from me again. If not, I remain your sincere well-wisher. You have provided me with the only happiness I have ever known.

And it was signed: Frankenstein (the Monster).

Hugo had scribbled the word "madness" across the paper.

The only remaining document I've been able to connect with this puzzling affair is a note written by my father of a psychic experiment he conducted with Victor Hugo several years later. It was not in the original file but in a notebook of my father's. Here is the relevant excerpt:

Last night Victor and I were alone. We talked of many things and I reminded him of the strange incident of the “monster” that had occurred to him several years past. He said he had had only one further communication from the creature. He then mentioned a letter that he received on the eve of the “Monster” departing back in time with the aid of a Doctor Faustus or Festus.

"Surely, it's a joke, Victor," I said.

"He seemed very sincere to me," he replied.

"Did you ever hear from him after that?"

"No–he must have got stuck in 1481–if he ever made it. I wish I could know more; the story has a strange fascination for me."

I suggested that, perhaps, we could channel back in time. At first, Victor was skeptical–then I told him I myself had attempted it and with a dream-like result. At that point, he became very agitated.

"You say you were there, with Quasimodo, on the roof of Notre-Dame and that he was just about to hurl himself off the roof to his death when–?"

"When Dracula appeared."

"Dracula. Is it possible?"

"Do you know who this Dracula is?"

"Dracula–is a vampire."

"A vampire! That would explain his ability to fly and revive the dead."

"So he turned Esmeralda and Quasimodo into vampires?"

"Yes–happy little vampires. Well, why not? Dracula needed servants and Quasimodo was very loyal. Esmeralda was dead anyway, and Quasimodo loved her. Yes. He's made them undead–but for them at least, it would have been better than death. Yes, yes–I see it..."

Victor had become very agitated and began pacing back and forth.

"I'd really like to know what happened when Frankenstein got there."

"That would certainly be interesting."

"Look here, Dumas, if you know how to do this thing–would you? Could you?"

"I gladly would–I'm not sure if I can. What I experienced last time seemed like a dream to me."

"I'll be here to help–to verify."

"In that case I shall try."

I sat down in an armchair and began to concentrate on the roof of Notre-Dame and to think about Quasimodo and Dracula. At first, nothing.

"I don't seem to be seeing much. Ah, wait!"

What I saw was the Monster and Doctor Faustus climbing up to the bell tower.

"Hurry, Doctor Faustus–we must not be late."

"Festus. I'm coming along but this is devilishly high."

"If you hadn't insisted on going to visit Weimar!"

"I wanted to see my old friends."

"I'm not paying you to see your old friends."

"We are here in time."

They had reached the top of the Cathedral. No one was around.

"There's no one here. We are too late."

"I think your friend Quasimodo is chasing Claude Frollo around still."

There was a noise and, turning, we all saw Quasimodo rushing after the terrified Frollo.They raced about for a while and Frollo lost his balance and fell off, clutching the water spout from which he dangled for quite a while before eventually falling with a terrible scream. But Quasimodo's attention was diverted toward the Place de Grève, where the executioner was busy hanging Esmeralda.

Suddenly, there was a huge beating of wings and Dracula landed like an elegant vulture behind Quasimodo. Quasimodo, unable to watch what was happening to Esmeralda, uttered a sob and prepared to hurl himself as Dracula said:

"Don't!"

At this moment, Frankenstein, in terrible agitation, rushed toward Dracula.

"He won't hurt you. I'll save you," the Monster blurted out.

He grabbed Dracula and pulled him away from Quasimodo, who looked on in astonishment and horror. Dracula drew his sword and brandished it at Frankenstein.

"Meddling fool! Don't interfere."

"I won't let you!"

Dracula lunged at Frankenstein, but the Monster parried his thrust with ease. Then, grabbing Dracula, he shoved him back.

"Very well. Have it your way," said the vampire lord. And Dracula suddenly vanished.

Frankenstein turned to Quasimodo who was looking at him with disbelief.

"Who are you? What have you done?"

"I'm Frankenstein. I'm a wretch like you. I've come to save you."

"Can you bring the dead to life?"

"No."

"Then, be cursed. You haven't saved me, you've ruined me. Oh, we were to be so happy as vampires–I can see it all now. All that good creature wanted to do for me. And you've ruined everything."

And Quasimodo hurled himself in tears at Frankenstein, who petted him gently, wiping his tears as the Hunchback pummeled him and kept telling the poor creature how he loved him.

I emerged from my trance.

"What a story, Alexander," said Hugo.

"A very strange story. Do you think it true, or just a figment of my imagination?"

The next page of the notebook was pulled out. It seemed as though there was more to the story, but evidently my father wanted to destroy all record of it. I have been unable to find any other documents that relate to this tragedy. Alexandre Dumas, fils.

Afterword

In trying to sum up the differences between the Frankenstein Monster and Quasimodo, the simplest approach may be simply to place the characters side-by-side.

Quasimodo is a sort of freak of nature, ugly, misshapen, but desperately in need of love and affection and capable of returning it, albeit in a primal, animal like way. He suggests that what we would call "retards" are not to be shunned but embraced, and treated with kindness and understanding. Thus it would seem Victor Hugo's view of nature is that it is basically good, even though in shape and form it may appear ugly. On the other hand, Quasimodo's–and Esmeralda's–unhappy fate suggests that despite the basic goodness of nature, life itself is often tragic.

Frankenstein is a freak not of nature but of man's creation. Of science and rationalism, according to Mary Shelley, and the tradition, of magic and human pride according to Charles Nodier. Although somewhat pitiful, in Shelley's version at least, Frankenstein proves intelligent–he reads a lot–and is to be pitied. But he is hard to embrace because he is vengeful, and violent. Ultimately, a much harsher monster than Hugo's. Shelley's approach to life is more bleak than truly tragic. Her monster survives and goes off into the Arctic. Nodier's version is more ambiguous, since we really don't know what happens next to the monster, but in both versions, he seems to be immortal.

ABOUT THE TRANSLATOR

Frank J. MORLOCK is an accomplished translator and has translated numerous plays by Alexandre Dumas including *Hamlet, Dr. Sturler's Experiment* (epilogue to *Comte Hermann*), *Napoleon Bonaparte, The Musketeers, The Barricades of Clichy, Lorenzino, The Vampire* a.k.a. *The Return of Lord Ruthven* (published by Black Coat Press), *Le Vingt-quatre février, Antony, La Reine Margot, Caligula, Urbain Grandier, Monte-Cristo, The Whites and the Blues, The Youth of Louis XIV, Kean* and many others.

Frank has also translated Victor Hugo's dramas, *Les Miserables, Ninety Three, Hans of Iceland* and *Notre-Dame de Paris* as well as numerous other plays such as Charles Nodier's *The Vampire* (published by Black Coat Press in *Lord Ruthven the Vampire*), Victor Darlay & Henry de Gorsse's *Arsène Lupin vs. Sherlock Holmes* (also poublished by Black Coat Press), *Madame Aubin* by Verlaine and *Signora Fantastici* by Madame de Stael. He also had three plays published by Rogue Publishing: Dumas' *The Man in The Iron Mask*, Victorien Sardou's *Young Figaro* and Maurice Leblanc and François de Croisset's original *Arsène Lupin.*

CPSIA information can be obtained at www.ICGtesting.com
Printed in the USA
LVOW072308241111

256388LV00001B/47/A